MANY WORLDS

MANY WORLDS

or, the simulacra

EDITED BY

CADWELL TURNBULL & JOSH EURE

NEW YORK

The story "Shock of Birth" was originally published in *Asimov's Science Fiction* (© 2020 by Cadwell Turnbull).

ISBN 978-1-7377184-3-7
Library of Congress Control Number: 2023902456

Editor
Meher Manda

Interior Layout and Design
Lantz Arroyo

Jacket Illustration
Le.BLUE

Jacket Design
Sarah Lopez

Printed and published in Brooklyn, New York by Radix Media.

Radix Media
522 Bergen Street
Brooklyn, New York 11217

radixmedia.org

ADVANCE PRAISE FOR MANY WORLDS

"*Many Worlds* brings the kind of brilliant, surreal, and deeply thought-provoking speculative fiction that will creep into your brain and under your skin and make you see and think differently about the world and the nature of reality. Together, this collection of stories forms an intricate and compelling kaleidoscopic vision of the fundamentally strange universe(s) we find ourselves in."

—Maria Haskins, Writer & Reviewer

"Time and place refuse to stand still in this beautiful collection of tales that examine the nature of reality from multiple levels and viewpoints. I was enthralled from start to finish and hope to read more stories set among and between these many worlds."

—Sheila Williams,
Editor at *Asimov's Science Fiction*

"A choral achievement—paranoid, touching, profound."

— Max Gladstone,
Hugo Award-Winning Author

"An ambitious experiment in fiction and storytelling exploring the nature of reality, truth, and self."

— A. C. Wise,
The Kissing Booth Girl and Other Stories

"In this anthology of stories set in a shared multiverse, Cadwell Turnbull and a search party of contemporary authors set out to explore the edges of the fantastic, an unsettling territory that seems like our world but not quite. It feels just like home."

— John Kessel,
Good News From Outer Space

Appendix F.

Collected here are complete transcriptions of each story referenced in this dissertation. They have been gathered from across the Simulacra and, taken together, they illustrate a burgeoning, if inchoate, awareness of the Simulacrum, emerging without coordination or communication across universes, across writers, across minds. This type of fictive engagement with the Simulacrum remains distressingly understudied, and this dissertation represents only a first, faltering step toward a better understanding of meaning-making by the denizens of the Simulacra who live in comparative ignorance of its workings.

All stories have been recalled via best Calibration practices.

Published by the Authority of the College of Multiple
Epistemologies and The Journal of Theoretical Epistemics

Published in adherence of Faculty Guidelines regarding
Consequence and Responsibility

Published in adherence of all Episcopal Requirements as
established during the Caughtlip Conventions

Published in adherence of all Episcopal Monitors'
Recommendations

Published with the intent to achieve greater understanding of
all Simulacral Phenomena

Published with the intent to expand the bounds of
Arcalumical Knowledge

CONTENTS

NOTES ON THE FORUM OF THE SIMULACRA

CADWELL TURNBULL

MEMBERS OF THE FORUM OF THE SIMULACRA believe that the world has been copied many times by an entity of unknown origin for an unknown purpose. (*Note: A god, a computer, a cosmic force?*) They call this entity the Simulacrum and its collection of worlds the Simulacra. The Simulacrum doesn't just copy the world, it adjusts it, adds things to the world, deletes other things. But its most terrifying power is its ability to alter meaning: to change what people care about or find interesting or the very relationships people have to things, to other people, to themselves.

CrayonsAreChanging (8.29.2018.8:57PM): I have a sister now. Just walked out of a room that wasn't there before. She's nice, I guess.

LuckYNo15 (4.30.2017.12:04AM): No one likes Caramel deLites? How the fuck does no one like Caramel deLites? Apparently people aren't buying them so they're discontinuing? What the fuck?

(*Note: Caramel deLites were awful. Almost as bad as Thin Mints. This is likely just group preferences masquerading as the Mandela Effect.*)

JUDAHS4 (6.6.2018.2.09AM): Pretty sure Montana had a population of over a million. Now it's 20,768. Weird. Also Hawai'i is its own country now.

It's impossible to tell if this is truly a mass delusion or a belief system inventing its own mythology. Older posts on the site appear to be no different than recent ones.

TheLostSheepKing (4.20.2007.6:06PM): The house I grew up in now belongs to a very polite old couple. They said they've been living there for 37 years. I'm only 21, returning for summer break. They invited me in and showed me pictures of their time in the house. Asked me if I was sure. I was until I saw the pictures. Anyone else experienced something like this?

Neverender (4.20.2007.6:08PM): I have. My childhood home is now a meadow. The town's name has changed.

Colleen (same time): I woke up this morning in a different house. Parents are the same but the dog is different. Her name is Snowball. She sits on the floor and stares at me and I don't like it.

Twenty-seven posts on the names of cities changing, all in the first day. By the following day, over a hundred posts about missing people or people with changed personalities or people whose roles have changed. Teachers becoming neighbors. Mothers becoming aunts. One incident of a husband of several years disappearing and turning up as the mailman. The speed of posts was very alarming, as was the genuine horror of them.

What's strange is that there's no origin post coining the term "Simulacrum." The concept exists without a referent, rules for the entity sprouting up like mushrooms, simultaneous. The earliest reference occurs over six years after the launch of the site. Stranger still, early posts are from members of the forum with no evidence of the site's creator.

TRutHsEeKR88 (10.04.2013.12:09AM): I'm pretty sure the Simulacrum has been altering the site. I tried to go back through old posts and it gave me a nosebleed. Anyone else getting nosebleeds?

To date there have been no responses to this post, though other members have described headaches, bouts of nausea, fainting spells. Always around perceived edits to reality.

Interestingly, only a few people without "edit experiences" have posted on the site. Their responses are what you might expect.

Simmons3 (7.23.2012.3:47PM): Are you guys for real?

Shinobi299 (9.11.2014.8:18AM): You people are nuts.

NguyenOcean (3.32.2016.7:09PM): This shit is really messing with my head. Please tell me you all are playing some elaborate joke?

Members of the forum respond to these inquiries with contempt.

"Another sheep has stumbled their way onto the forum."

"Fuck off, sheeple."

Or philosophical musings:

CumulusTen (2.14.2014.11:22PM): "Is it possible that the Simulacrum sends people here every once in a while to mock us? How do we know that what we know isn't also to mock us? What if we wake up tomorrow and forget everything ?"

It does feel genuinely eerie that more people don't visit the site, but perhaps this is my own obsession speaking. Most people probably dismiss the site entirely, and why wouldn't they? There are only a handful of active users at any given time. Private conversations with members have proved fruitless; everyone is fully committed to the ruse or they truly believe what they are saying. (*Perhaps convince someone to meet in person?*)

I've been researching the site for months(?) and still have not gotten any closer to understanding why it exists. With each day I gain less clarity, having forgotten why I started this research in the first place. I write these reports and journals and notes and leave them all over my apartment with no idea as to why I am writing them or who I might want to read them. Each note begins the same but morphs as I continue, until the thing before me fills me with horror. These notes are all punctuated by the same symbol: a circle with arms, a serpent around an apple, an all-seeing eye? I never remember drawing the symbol, and have difficulty describing it. When I sleep, I see it in my dreams. A door opens in front of me, and through it I can see another world, a cityscape with a massive tower, the symbol carved into its front. And a young woman whose features shift like claymation putty. Her hand is outstretched to mine, but when I try to grab hold of her and step through, everything turns white, and the scene resets. This other world is always the same and I can feel a sense of longing every time I see it. After several attempts, the woman says, *I keep losing track of you*, and her voice is so painfully familiar that despair fills me to bursting and I wake up screaming.

(*Please save yourself, my love.*)

Some of the members of the forum believe that the true world still exists, unaltered by the Simulacrum. Most members, however, believe the true world is forever lost.

They return to places that have been altered like orphans.

Neverender (6.32.2020.5:09AM): I visit the field often. I look at those flowers and I imagine that they are the people of my hometown, swaying with the wind like dancers at a celebration that will never end.

The ones who believe in the untouched world also believe in other worlds beyond a veil no one can see, but are accessible through the ritual of performing unique actions: holding one's breath for a minute and thirty seconds, jumping from a great height, eating cake on the fourth of July. They believe these mechanisms of travel are gifted to them by the Simulacrum itself, both demon and god in their strange mythology.

Here is the earliest instance I could find regarding the subject of traveling between worlds, transcribed in its entirety:

FlowersJustFlowers (11.22.2013.11:58PM): It is my fault she is gone and it is all my fault

Neverender (11.23.2013.12:27AM): I'm so sorry you've lost someone. It never gets easier, but please don't blame yourself. The Simulacrum is the only one to blame.

FlowersJustFlowers (11.23.2013.12:34AM): You don't understand I came from another world I did Terrible Things to stay here and now this world keeps shifting around me likes and I did this she is gone and it is all my fault.

Neverender (11.23.2013.12:36AM): What are you talking about?

TheLostSheepKing (11.23.2013.12:40AM): Which part don't you understand?

Neverender (11.23.2013.12:41AM): Sorry, I was confused for a second. It's late here.

JstPssngThrgh001 (11.23.2013.12:45AM): You said you came from another world FlowersJustFlowers. I'm curious about your mode of travel. Do you mind sharing?

FlowersJustFlowers (11.23.2013.12:50AM): Every fifth and seventh blink in an alternating pattern full stop

TheLostSheepKing (11.23.2013.12:52AM): Oh god. That's hellish.

JstPssngThrgh001 (11.23.2013.1:03AM): That is unusual. Reminds me of the musical meter. If it's true, the repetition suggests design.

TheLostSheepKing (11.23.2013.1:07AM): Or a cruel sense of humor. That's a terrible time signature.

BENthoven__420__69 (11.23.2013.1:25AM): I mean, it's more that it's not really a meter unto itself, as 5/7 would be indistinguishable from 5/8, which would be much easier to read. Alternating bars of 5/8 and 7/8 would make sense, but that's not something that I think many people would immediately think of if presented with a pattern of five then seven. A bar of 5/7 could make sense in the context of another time signature conceivably, but denominators that are odd numbers are vanishingly rare. A septuplet is a septuplet by virtue of the fact that seven of them fit in whatever musical space you assign them, but if you want them to be the base rhythmic unit a bar is measured in their function as a septuplet immediately vanishes; 7/7 is just 7/8, and 5/7 is just 5/8 (or 5/4 or 5/2, depending on whether you're using eighth notes or quarter notes or half notes in the notation). No, I think we can safely rule out "time signature" as an explanation.

TheLostSheepKing (11.23.2013.1:17AM): Awesome. Thanks for the explanation. Totally needed all that.

Cartographer218 (11.23.2013.2:30AM): Yesterday I was walking down the street at midday when a young woman passed me. I thought I recognized her so I turned around. When I did, she was farther than I thought she should be, like the sidewalk had expanded between us. I considered calling out but thought it would be strange; I didn't know her by name even if I knew her. But she also stopped, and then she turned to face me in much the same way I had moments before. We watched each other as the crowd moved between us. She said, *Mother?* and rushed up to me. I tried to turn away, but she had me by the arm. She said, *Listen, we have to leave this world. It's dangerous.* I shook my head. She sounded insane. She said, *Mother, your scent keeps vanishing and I keep losing track of you.* I began to tremble. I don't know why. She asked me if I recognized her. I told her to please let me go. She looked around frantically. People were staring at us. She started again, her voice lower. She said, *This world is unstable. I can get us out, but you need to come with me now.* I asked her if she was from the forum. It didn't seem like a stupid question at the time. The woman began to cry. She called me mother again, but did not finish her statement; the sun came out from behind a building behind us and when it hit her eyes the irises changed from dark brown to a startling green. It had to be a trick of the light, but her skin brightened too, from copper to pale white, the tears drying on her cheeks. My head started to hurt and I felt faint. The strange young woman looked around again, but this time she seemed lost. She turned to me and asked me if I knew where the Copley T-stop was. I smiled and pointed the way.

(*I am sorry. I need to lie down again.*)

THE PHANTOM OF THE MARLEE VALLEY HIGH AUDITORIUM FOR THE PERFORMING ARTS

THEODORE McCOMBS

MARLEE VALLEY, COLO: THE LAST TIME ANYONE saw Stella Baird, 17, was at her high school's spring show. It was the show's final piece, a sequence of intricate group dances called the Gurdjieff Movements; she'd been rehearsing for weeks. In the wings, Stella and her friends caught their breath and listened excitedly for their fourth entrance cue. The next thing anyone knew, Stella was gone.

Baird is Marlee Valley's fiftieth disappearance in eight years. All of the missing are high school students, and they all disappeared just before, after, or during the high school's spring show. In 2015 and 2018, students even disappeared while on stage. "There was one of those big group turns where everyone's sort of hard to tell apart," said Eagle County Deputy Sheriff Davis Perry, who was in the audience both times. "And when the formation settled, their spots were empty."

The Sheriff's Office does not comment on ongoing investigations, but confirmed that one year later, there have been no arrests in Baird's case—or in any of the other cases. Baird's father, like many Marlee Valley parents, long ago resigned himself to this: "There are never any leads," said Ed Baird, 46.

But Baird's mother thinks school authorities aren't doing enough. June Baird already lost her nephew, Tanner, in 2013, and has since made herself something of an activist over her hometown's rash of disappearances. "They all happen—every single one—around the spring show's final act, the Gurdjieff Movements," she said. "That's not a coincidence, that's a law of nature."

∝

Laws of nature dominate Marlee Valley, a tiny outpost of houses and grazing land tucked off the Rockies' Interstate 70 corridor, in the shadow of massive ridges that keep their snowcaps year-round. It's tricky to breathe at this altitude, and there's a strange pollen in the air that makes the eyes water. An aggressive loosestrife roots into sidewalk cracks and bursts open the concrete. There are two days in spring when the valley flashes purple with their blossom, and residents say the mountains look almost alive in this color. When the breeze ripples the loosestrife, they seem to thrum and breathe.

As June Baird tells it, her nephew Tanner never used to pay much attention to this high-mountain splendor—he was a typical teenager. But as he rehearsed for the 2013 spring show, he got a "funny, big-eyed look to him."

He wandered absent-mindedly, taking the wrong streets home—in a town so small, few streets can be wrong—or stopping to stare at a solitary piñon pine on the ridge. June remembers asking him, "How was school today?" and being answered with a twenty-minute speech on the creation of the Sun and planets out of accumulated interstellar dust, billions of years ago. Some of it sounded like Greek, a language Tanner never learned.

After the show, June Baird waited with Tanner's parents outside the stage door with the other families. It was just the second year of the disappearances; people remembered the town's tragic losses the year before, but no one suspected it would turn into a pattern. "No one even told him to be careful," June said. She remembers that half hour after the show ended, that happily wasted time at the stage door, as her last easy wait.

June Baird is a striking, elegant mountain woman, whose typical outfit is a checkered fleece jacket over a stylish silk blouse. She runs a home daycare and proudly displays ten years of flawless inspection reports in her front hall. The family room is a toddler's paradise of bright-colored blocks, illustrated books, picture puzzles, and manipulables, and everything, from the covered electrical outlets to the state-of-the-art princess house, declares this space a hermetically sealed "clean room" of childhood innocence. But when June enters Stella's empty bedroom, her shoulders sag and she hugs her chest. That worst-case scenario she's dreaded for six years has finally happened.

"I failed her," June said. Not just in keeping Stella safe, but in providing her the kind of world in which teenagers angst over trivial dramas—volleyball tryouts, itchy prom dresses, and embarrassing crushes. In June Baird's day, high-schoolers didn't have to worry about active-shooter drills. Now she runs those drills in her daycare.

It's hard to think of any precaution June Baird hasn't tried over the years, but now she blames herself for not monitoring her daughter's video diaries: like many Gen Zs, Stella had a YouTube channel. The last time June checked, about six months before Stella's disappearance, it was "standard girl stuff"—fumbling makeup tutorials and the occasional thoughtful riff on her history class readings. But in the month leading up to the spring performance, the channel shows her posting longer, rambling videos on geology and cosmology: on the "Laramide orogeny," mountain-building, dark cloud constellations, and cosmic time. She started to sound like her cousin Tanner, in other words.

The piece Tanner and Stella performed in their spring shows—the piece that's performed every year as the last act—is the Gurdjieff Movements, a progression of sacred dances developed by George Ivanovich Gurdjieff in the 1910s. Gurdjieff, a mystic philosopher of Armenian-Greek origins, claimed to have collected the dances over his travels in Russia, the Caucasus, Tibet, and India, and synthesized them into a movement practice calibrated to wake the dancer into a higher state of consciousness. The rhythmic, almost clockwork motions, scored to a hypnotic piano and danced in grid formations, bear names like 'Triads in Pairs: Complexity in Simplicity' or 'Canon of Six Measures: Cosmic Dance.' Sixteen students dance the Movements every year, dressed incongruously in the skirts and tall, brown *sikke* hats of Turkish whirling dervishes.

June Baird wants the school to suspend performances of the Gurdjieff Movements, which she points out are the common link across the disappearances. The first student vanished the year the drama teacher introduced the Movements into the spring show and have continued every year since—and always in the rough window of time the Gurd-jieff Movements are performed. In 2006, the school board voted 'No' on June's request. "The decision was made to defer on programming to the Drama Department," said Marlee Valley High's principal, Sheila Glover.

◌

Principal Glover's classrooms are full of photographs taped up by bereaved schoolmates, and emptied desks record the missing in carvings on their undersides: "Kendrik was here," "Lisa 4evah." Glover observed that "small towns are drying up all over the country," and was resistant to the idea her school was any different.

But county records show Marlee Valley's substance abuse rates for teens is higher than state and national averages. Only 23% of its graduates secure a job or attend secondary education in their first years after high school; 45% qualify for public assistance. Ironically, kids who work on their families' ranches or small businesses from age 10 up find less opportunity when they try to leave the nest. County officials have made strides in vocational training, but the bigger problems facing Marlee Valley teens seem intractable. "We're always asking for thoughts and prayers," said Deputy Sheriff Perry.

At a candlelight vigil, the First Congregation of the Rocky Mountains is packed with well-wishers in wool sweaters and down vests. The tables bear portrait photos of teens in sports uniforms and Sunday suits, framed by flower sprays of that same wild loosestrife. As the candles are lit, there's a murmur of excitement and consternation. In the middle of the crowd, one spot is painfully bright, as if there are a hundred candles held together in one armful. No one seems to be responsible for the bright spot, which makes its way slowly up to the altar through the crowd of attendees. People start shouting questions to it or even trying to push away, but there's always still a huddle of limbs and shoulders surrounding it. When the bright spot reaches the front of the church, the parting crowd reveals nothing, produces no one, and the service continues.

Marlee Valley High School students have a name for this kind of phenomenon, which tends to crop up around the annual disappearances: The Too-Many. That's when there seem to be more people than are really there when you count. There's an arm left over, or a face that doesn't belong to anyone when you match them all up. In 2015, when

Eric Romero disappeared on stage, one dancer said she saw an extra leg, as if there was some unseen person standing behind him.

Then there's the Heap: a pile of props, boxes, dress forms, or other equipment tied up in dark blankets, which doesn't belong where it is: blocking the lockers in a hallway, or in the girls' bathrooms. "Everyone sort of sees it and doesn't see it," explained one student, who asked not to be identified. No one touches or mentions it—until the next day, by which point another handful of classmates have gone missing.

Matthew Heller, the high school's dance and drama teacher, even saw the Heap moving one year. During intermission, he was looking for a lost prop in between the two layers of heavy stage curtains. He had a flashlight, but the beam could only go a few feet into the dense folds of the curtains. "I saw a large figure wrapped in black stage blankets, moving between the inner and outer curtains," he said, "tall, tied with nylon rope, and leaning to one side, sort of staggering, like it wasn't used to walking." He said he chased it, thinking it might be the kidnapper, but lost it in the dark.

Heller doesn't think the Gurdjieff Movements have anything to do with the disappearing kids, however. Neither does Ed Baird: "That's June's drum to bang," he said. As of printing, the Gurdjieff Foundation has declined to comment for this story.

ↈ

Deputy Sheriff Perry, in the meantime, has deployed every safety measure at his disposal. There are law officers in the wings with taser guns. He puts on a training for the kids every year: there's a buddy system, a line-of-sight rule, a checkpoint rule, a hotline. "Everyone's been a real hero about it," he said. But he can't say it's prevented any one disappearance. Perry defends his office's failure to make even a single arrest over eight years of cases: "Making any arrest on this evidence would be the failure."

Still, Perry won't cancel the spring show or the Gurdjieff Movements, saying it's not his decision.

No one has a satisfactory explanation for the Gurdjieff Movements' popularity in this proudly conventional mountain town. To an outsider, Gurdjieff's religious philosophy—a murky, appropriative blend of Sufism, Russian Orthodox ritual, and New Agey Spiritualism—seems too arcane for rural Colorado, and especially for its high schoolers' young age. Principal Glover acknowledges that the Movements force students to confront mature questions about life and death, their belief in a higher power, and the meaning we bring to our time on Earth. "We're not about to treat those questions as something to be feared, though."

Glover, a generation older than June Baird, remembers her high school years differently, and has little patience for nostalgia: "It wasn't active-shooter drills, but we had nuclear strike drills. I remember being told the only thing to do for an atomic blast was to get under our desks."

Heller echoed this sentiment, listing off the things that already make the world a fearful place for his students: rising cost of living, dwindling job prospects, gun violence, environmental degradation. "What I can offer them," Heller said, "through poetry, literature, and yes, dance, are lives a little bigger than they were yesterday." Adolescence is a key moment of awakening, Heller observed, when one starts to view the world critically and ask if there's more to it. "It's a time of veil-lifting."

Still, the students know there's *something* to be feared. "You wonder who it's going to be this year," said Tabby Jessen, 16, a senior. Every year it wasn't her, the anxiety got worse. "You feel bad, because you're relieved it was them, not you," she explained. "And it keeps happening, again, again, again."

Devon Kostick, 19, has graduated and works the front desk at a Vail ski resort. He called his experience in Marlee Valley High "intense." Asked if he feels safe now, he replied, "No one should feel safe." He blinked slowly, then repeated wondrously: "Safe?"

Both Jessen and Kostick support June Baird's activism, but expressed resignation about changing any minds. "People just keep on doing what they're doing," said Jessen. Drawing any kind of connection between the disappearances and the Gurdjieff Movements leads to the adults shouting them down, or condescendingly accusing them of "Denver talk."

"It's always been out of our hands," said Jessen.

☡

The land in Marlee Valley is mottled in ice and covered in dying lodgepole pines, whose graying trunks and skeletal branches line the freeway all the way to Idaho Springs. The Rocky Mountains' peaks stand tall, white, and silent. "Look at them too long and you start to feel like a fly on the back of a gigantic divine bull," Stella said, in her last uploaded YouTube journal. "Something so huge and long-lived, it's only your smallness and briefness that lets you stay on its back. You start to feel like if you jumped too hard, you might not land. Like there's this—this dignity easing you off the top of the world." In the video, she pauses and stares at a point above the frame, and her awkward, careful features loosen into a smile of recognition. "Other times, I feel like I myself am the top of the world and everything's about to fall off of me." She describes "mountains inside of me, bigger than anything," and then the video cuts off.

But to June Baird, nothing can be bigger than the shame of fifty missing kids. Asked how she'd respond to her critics, she looked ahead, as if into a camera lens, and said: "Not one more."

Kostick offers a different motto: "Ask yourself, would you live your life any differently if you knew you were going to make it out of high school alive, or you weren't?" He was surprised to realize how much he'd do the same, he said. He then hesitated.

"Just—don't touch the Heap."

A SKILLFUL IMPOSTOR

REBEKAH BERGMAN

S HE WENT TO BED IN MARCH AND WOKE UP in April. It was exhausting how a new month would start before she'd grown used to the old. This month, in particular, began with all things called into question. The first of April, a day for scrutinizing. She resigned herself to read the newspaper carefully over her breakfast. To take nothing at face value. Everything with a grain of salt. But what did the date matter, really? What we believe is truth can always be someone else's idea of a joke.

The word scrutinize was the first thing she scrutinized. She did it without meaning to. It was such a very odd word. Those opening consonants, how they forced the lips to purse. Scrutinize. She said it aloud and her husband muttered back in his sleep. He did not yet know what the day was. Lucky man. Or did he? She remembered to doubt.

So today she would try hard to second guess. Most days, this was not the case. Most days, she tried not to peel back the layers of reality and peer beneath. But this day was different. She'd read once—and where had she read it?—of a woman who'd become convinced that her husband was not her husband. He was instead, she'd said, a skillful impostor. How did she even think to think that? In any case, the not-husband knew her husband's walk and the length of his showers and the way he chewed his food. He mimicked it all, the not-wife said. Imagine that, she thought now, and she imagined it. She looked at her husband and found it quite easy to imagine it, actually.

What she could not believe was the ending of that story. What the not-wife had done about the impostor. She had done nothing. She hadn't looked for her real husband or kicked the impostor out of her home. She'd lived with the not-husband for over a decade. She said she'd grown used to him. They'd grown used to each other. Eventually, she said, they had fallen in love.

AND SO, WHAT DO YOU KNOW?

K.W. ONLEY

TWO LITTLE BLACK GIRLS AND THEIR MOM WALK with purpose into Takoma Park Station, first stop in Maryland, last stop before Washington D.C. For these Maryland girls—suburban girls—getting on the Metro is an irregular treat and always a prelude to adventure. Electric-static scents fill the girls' nostrils inside the little station where the fare machines huff hot air and wait to be fed. On the platform, while they wait for the train, Mom's phone chirps and a woman starts talking. "Hey Cheryl? You on your way?"

Mom reaches into her purse to take out the thick black square and press the side button that makes it chirp back. She holds it to her lips. "Yep. And on time."

Anita and Sheena know what the chirps mean. They step away from Mom and choose not to listen. Sheena bobs her head from side to side, making the plastic beads at the end of her little braids click. She smiles in delight, the width of each swing getting wider, the click and clatter getting louder. Anita smiles but doesn't participate, knowing she is much too old now to play with her hair beads. But Little Sister, go ahead, swing your beads. Be free and happy.

Mom places a hand on Sheena's shoulder but gives Anita the Look. "Ladies, we know how to wait."

They are ladies who know how to wait. They are ladies who know a lot of things. Sometimes, when they are together and away from Mom, they wonder if their whole life is just a long lesson in knowing. They hope the answer was no. Anita thinks the answer might be yes.

As the little sister, Sheena gets the window seat on the train. Sheena is in Third Grade, a sturdy nine-year-old, but she still gets extra privileges. Mom assures Anita that Sheena gets no more than she does, but Anita knows what she sees and knows what she knows. She is tall enough now to still see out the window even when sitting in the second seat, so she's not mad about it like she used to be. Mom sits in the seats behind them, watchful of the other adults on the train. Sheena kicks her legs as the train slides into motion.

"I think, sometimes, that I'll always have a Nintendo in my house," Sheena declares.

Anita smiles. What a thought. The world passes by the window in a blur of colors: green streaking into brown, into gray, into blue sky and puffy clouds above the rooftops.

"Do you think you'll always have a Nintendo?"

Anita nods her head, actually thinking about it. Of course she'll always have a Nintendo. They love their Nintendo 64 and they are girls who know how to share. They aren't supposed to be thinking about their Christmas list yet, but the new Zelda is coming out soon. Did she dare to ask Mom for it? Maybe Special Sheena, with her extra little sister privileges, can do it without getting into trouble.

They ride on the Red Line on their way to transfer at Metro Center. The world looks so different on the railroad tracks, like seeing buildings in only their underwear: overflowing dumpsters, abandoned shopping carts, rust-streaked loading docks, broken lawn chairs nestled around hole-pocked grills, and every surface covered with layers of graffiti. Anita particularly loves reading the flamboyant bubble letters of competing artists. She idly wonders why Joe Cool always uses white, while Wize Joe always uses red, and how do they manage to get to such high places where there are no steps or ladders? Most of the stuff is just names on a wall. Sometimes, there is something interesting like a face or a flower or a curse word.

The train comes to a stop before Catholic U Station. "Thank you for your patience. The train will enter the station momentarily," the train's computer voice announces. Outside the wide window is a foot path under an overpass. Anita can faintly hear the movement of traffic on the bridge overhead. The walls of the overpass hold her attention. Someone painted the B-word in big, bold blue letters on the water-stained concrete wall. Anita stares at it and suppresses a laugh because she knows Mom won't approve and she probably isn't supposed to know what that word is anyway. But she does know. All the girls in Seventh Grade know. She knows how good it feels to use it sometimes.

Under the B-word is a clump of words, written in plain black spray-paint with no other flourishes: "Change is gonna come," says one clump and then right next to it, in a different color and style, is "ask already so we can receive!" Anita leans in to stare at the clumps of words. Just under them, someone else has written, "Will you know it when you see it?"

"What are you looking at?" Sheena asks, looking at Anita and then looking back out the window, leaning into the glass.

"Nothi—"

"What's that big word right there? Is that…Oh! Is that the B-Word?" Sheena squeals, her joy slicing through the polite quiet of the train car. Anita's mouth drops open. Little sisters ruin everything.

Mom leans in between them, her whisper sharp in their ears. "Ladies, we know how to ride the train!"

They are ladies who know how to ride the train. Anita gives her sister the side-eye, peeved to be in trouble. Sheena shrinks a little and looks down at the floor. The train starts moving and Anita watches the B-word and the rest of the bubble letters turn into a blur of colors. She thinks about change and wonders why anyone would want it. Change is a word just as bad as any cuss to Anita's mind. Her right hand wants to reach for the new training bra strap cutting into the soft meat of her shoulder while her left hand wants to reach for her midsection, rubbing away a phantom cramp. Change, she decides, is a B-word.

♻

At the top of the escalator at Federal Triangle, as the station entrance opens to the empty street, a woman squats next to a pink granite wall, her belongings around her, a sign resting at her feet: "Your change please." A white man walking ahead of Anita reaches into his pocket, pulls out a couple of coins, and flicks them into a small bowl next to the sign. A group of people walking in a cluster pass by next, one of them close enough to trip on the woman's feet before kicking her bowl with a shriek and cuss. The woman shrinks back a bit, making herself smaller in her corner, pulling the bowl in and losing the chance to collect more change. A couple of coins come out in the disturbance, the chime as they hit the pavement ringing through the entrance. Sheena lets go of Mom's hand to run over to get the coins, dashing between the walking people who haven't slowed their stride. Anita does the same. When they drop the coins back in the woman's bowl, Sheena says "sorry."

Mom has stopped and moved aside. People pass by without noticing. Anita waits for a reminder of what they're supposed to know. Mom just starts walking instead.

They step onto 12th street and face lots of white columns. Federal Triangle is home to statues of women who point toward nothing in particular or hold symbols that probably have deep meaning to someone Anita doesn't know. Like the rest of the crowd that emerges from the station, Mom turns toward Pennsylvania Avenue and the Taste of D.C.

The three of them walk at a steady pace with a growing crowd of excited, hungry people. This is an everybody kind of event—anxious white couples with strollers, gaggles of slick-haired white men in button-down shirts and shorts, Black families and Brown families with happy children skipping along, and entrepreneurs of all colors looking for opportunity and attention. Not all D. C. events draw a crowd this diverse. Food, Anita guesses, really is for everyone.

The approaching crowd walks with their eyes straight forward toward the tents, the rising smoke, and the waving movement of the crowd already there. Echoing off the textured gray walls of the Federal buildings is the sound of go-go and laughter, and so many spices all coming together to make one perfect smell.

Not far from the sidewalk, a little dog sits next to a mound of fabric and a collection of plastic bags with yellow happy faces on them full of indiscernible items. The dog yips at the passersby, not loudly, but enough to draw Anita and Sheena's attention. Sitting on a tattered sleeping bag, faded and green, a younger man, locs coming down to his shoulders, sits with a sign of Sharpie-black bubble letters on cardboard: "I need change!" Anita lets her eyes draw up from the man and the dog, out toward the gray-white steps of the government buildings on either side of the street. Among their high, imposing columns are clusters of gray and black and faded colors, sometimes accompanied by trash bags or collapsible hand carts. Anita slows to get a good look, but someone steps on the back of her shoe.

"We know how to be on time, ladies."

Mom increases her pace, pulling Sheena along.

☯

The Taste of D.C. is a colorful cacophony of vendor tents. Around them meander a crowd of thousands. Balloons float beside fluttering flags of the nations represented in chef-crafted cuisine. The white Channel 4 tent stands in the middle of all of the smoke-filled restaurant tents and happy feasters. People waiting for autographs and swag bags stand in a happy line around the tent chatting, eating, and enjoying themselves. As one of the bosses at the television station, Mom has to be at the tent for a couple of hours to ensure things run smoothly. The girls don't mind at all because the Taste of D.C. is their favorite event to come into the city for. A little work now, delicious food later. That's a deal Sheena and Anita know is good.

When they reach the large event tent with the Channel 4 logo on all sides, Mom greets a couple of co-workers and signals for Anita and Sheena to enter the tent. In front of the tent are a couple of the famous people who are on TV every night. They wave at Mom and wave at Anita and Sheena. Mom reminds them to wave back. In line, people who are probably otherwise rational and normal bounce on their toes and fidget with excitement as they wait to meet the TV people. Anita watches them while Mom speaks with a few colleagues before pointing her and Sheena to the back of the tent.

In the back, which is the majority of the tent, are boxes full of folders, papers, photographs, plastic frisbees, and little plastic Working4You bags to put them all in.

Mom looks at Anita. "You are girls who know what to do."

They are. They've done it many times before.

"You need to fill this box before we leave and go get somethin' to eat," Mom says, pointing into a tall box. An adult ducks in, smiles at Mom and says "Hey Cheryl" before leaning into the box, taking an armful of bags out, and slipping back into the sunlight again. Mom gives Anita a smile, then goes to the front of the tent where the rest of the adults stand together.

Sheena ventures over to the big box, then starts looking over what the assembly line was before. Anita joins her, opening up boxes and placing stacks of headshots and flyers in their places for easy stuffing. They sit down and get started. Sheena has magic fingers that always seemed to open those plastic bags with no trouble and no licking.

Around them, on the other side of the tent walls, people converse and laugh while chefs cook and grill. Behind them, adults come in and out of the work area, some getting more bags to give away to people; others to have a quick conversation before heading back out to the front. Anita and Sheena work diligently, filling the tall box slowly. From time to time, Anita looks over her shoulder to glance at the adults coming into the space.

A tall woman, brown-skinned and honey-kissed in the undertones, box braids going all the way down to her hips, slips in without Anita's noticing. Perfume, something deep, fruity and rich, takes over the smell of the tent, overpowering the rich scents of a world's worth of food around them, which is what draws Anita's attention and turns her around.

"There you are! Cheryl's girls! The girls, I'm told, who know!"

Sheena hasn't broken her rhythm, so she sucks her teeth at Anita when she realizes that big sister has come to a full stop. Anita barely notices—she has turned fully around to look the woman over: spotless blue Adidas on her feet, cuffed overalls that show a little ankle, a short-sleeved blue and yellow midriff showing just a little bit of skin on the side of the overalls, and an elaborate lace choker around her neck.

Sheena finally comes to a stop and looks the woman over, too. "Hello," Sheena says in a measured, trained way. They both know how to talk to Mom's co-workers. But this woman doesn't really look like any co-worker of Mom. Sheena is leaning back and looking toward the front of the tent. Anita leans forward, to be the big sister in front.

"Why y'all lookin' like that? Your mama didn't mention me? I'm here to interview you!"

Anita hasn't had the opportunity to give an adult The Look before, but this is a time to do so. "Interview?"

The woman takes four graceful strides to cross the space between them, which makes Sheena squeak and lean closer to Anita. She stops before she gets too close, though, and waves at them. "My name is Nikki. I'm with the Department of Continuity. Your Mama and I went to Hampton together. She and I are good friends."

Anita thinks through her memory of Mom's "Hampton Friends" and cannot recall a Nikki. And she thinks through her list of government departments that she knows from school and can't recall a Department of Continuity.

"My job is to catalog the things we need, the things we don't, and the things we can stand to see changed," Nikki continues. "Haven't you ever noticed that things just *change* sometimes? We can't really predict it, but we know that changes happen. We're looking for ways to control it. Or control the experience of it. As a country, you know? It's chaos when we don't." She waves her hands around her in wide circle. "This right here, our mutual reality, is just another construct, ladies. I think you know what I mean. You are girls who know a lot."

Sheena leans in a bit, peering around Anita's shoulder to listen more closely. Anita leans back, though, the not-rightness filling in more spaces of the knowing in her gut. Neither girl speaks, and Nikki lets the silence between them grow, her shimmering lips curling in a warm smile.

It takes a few breaths before Sheena says impatiently, "And *so?*"

Nikki laughs. "And *so*, precious girl! *And so*, I'm here to interview you! I need to know what you know! What you know helps us define the meaning of now and the meaning of later. I catalog your knowing. Your knowing anchors our knowing. There are all sorts of people who know. Y'all are among them! I'm not going to say too much, but when we next experience a Change Time, that means what we know will get little…tweaks. Or big ones. We never know until after it's done. And it happens more often than you think. It's hard to explain, but *it happens*. Just believe me! So we keep a catalog of what has been and what has been changed. We accept some changes. We resist or deny others. Sometimes, we get to *redefine* the changes as best we can, based on our catalog of knowing. And before, you see, it was only certain people who got to decide what we know, but we've learned that a small group of people *can't* know everything. So that's why I work at the Department of Continuity. That's why

I get to interview you. I think you deserve to know. I work with your Mom to make sure you do!"

Anita shakes her head. She feels Sheena shift in her seat. The woman is speaking words, in English, but they don't make any sense. They aren't words that normal adults would say. Mom wouldn't let someone like this talk to them alone. If she knows anything at all, she knows *that* at least. But what she doesn't know is how to get herself and Sheena away. She decides to be simple and polite. "No thank you, ma'am. I don't think we want to be interviewed."

This Nikki person nods, something like understanding on her face. "Yup. You two be knowin'. Y'all are perfect. Your mama trained you well! Home training is a gift that will keep on giving, ladies!" Anita watches her and flashes her eyes to the tent flap leading to the front. Where is Mom? Worse comes to worst, she and Sheena can scramble under one of the tent walls.

"I just want to know," Nikki says, taking a small notebook and a pen out of her pocket, "what do little Black girls know that nobody else knows?"

"That...nobody else...knows?" Anita repeats. What a question.

Nikki nods, flipping her little notebook open and turning the pages with a finger. "Yes. What do you know, Anita? When it comes to this world, this universe, this timeline of life, what do you know? What should continue? What is one thing that must change?"

Anita shakes her head. Sheena does too, her beads clicking and clattering in Anita's ear. Behind Nikki, but obscured by a tent wall, someone laughs loudly. The din of the crowd seems to increase around the tent.

Nikki holds her pen poised. She watches the two of them with soft eyes that read patience and warmth. She looks so relaxed, so in control, and her outfit is so fly. Anita still wants to be her, even as she wants to run away from her. She wants to ask her a question, to know what she knows. And those thoughts bring other thoughts—about all the things she has to do between now and however old you have to be to become that cool.

The thought makes her back itch where the stupid clasp for her stupid bra rubs against her skin.

Nobody talks. Nikki doesn't do anything. Anita doesn't want to be the first to do something. The three of them stay still. The tent walls move in and out like waves on a beach day. Shadows darken and fade in the wall fabric.

"I know how to wait," Sheena says shyly. She leans against Anita, the weight of her pushing them both forward even though Anita doesn't want to move any closer.

Nikki smiles and starts writing. "What do you mean?"

"Uhm…" Sheena curls around Anita. Anita sighs. Little Sister, what have you done?

Nikki doesn't seem to mind the silence. She locks eyes with Anita. Anita shrugs, looking away.

"Like, there is this one girl, Kima. She's in my class," Sheena starts, her voice rising in that way kids do when they start a story. "One time, she got impatient with Mrs. Williams when it was her turn to play Math Munchers but Mrs. Williams gave Lila the turn instead. And so Kima got mad. She had waited a long time. I remember because I spent some of that time with her. But Lila went anyway, even though we all knew it was unfair. So Kima decided she wasn't going to do any more floor time and she went to her seat to go color. And Mrs. Williams told Kima to come back three times, but she didn't. So Mrs. Williams called down to the office. And Mr. Connors came and took Kima to the office and Kima wasn't allowed back in school for the rest of the week." She took a breath. "So now, when someone takes my turn, I just wait. And I don't say anything. I'm just quiet and nobody notices me and that's ok."

Nikki writes it all down, nodding slowly. "And do you think all girls like you know how to wait?"

Sheena puffs her cheeks. Anita hears it in her ear, hot air eventually hitting the back of her neck. "I wish Kima did…I think she does now. We all do. Me, and Kima, and Natalie, and Gayle…"

Nikki nods and keeps writing. Sheena doesn't say anything else. Anita thinks about what her sister said. She thinks about how much she agrees with her—being noticed usually means getting into trouble or hearing a lecture or being sent somewhere. Better to get by unseen. She knows plenty of girls who haven't figured it out yet and get into trouble because of it. There are plenty of things that she wants, but not all of those things are worth the trouble or the energy or the fight, even if it means school might be better for her and her friends. She's a girl who knows that change is painful to make.

But she also thinks about how it makes her feel to hear her sister say those words. They sink in and she feels like drooping or standing up straighter. She can't really tell. She wants to do both at once.

Nikki locks eyes on her. "I see your face. What are you thinking about?"

Anita knows how to fix her face. "Nothing."

Nikki smiles. "Oh, you're good. Okay. Do you know how to wait, too? Should little Black girls continue to know how to wait?"

Anita nods, but then she has a thought. "I think waiting is one of the things we know."

Nikki writes, silent.

And Anita can't stop herself from thinking more. "I'm not sure we should know. Why doesn't Lila know how to wait, but Kima has to know? Why do I have to know? Why does Sheena have to know? Maybe who should have to wait and who shouldn't should change."

Nikki nods and writes. Sheena breathes behind Anita. She doesn't say anything. Anita thinks she feels Sheena shiver a little.

Nikki lifts her pen and looks up. "Good, sure. Well, so? If *you* could ask for one change in the world and *know* that it would be changed…what would you ask for, Anita? Will you tell me next time I see you?"

Anita frowns. What a question. What a thought.

"Ladies, how are we doing back here?" Mom calls from the front of the tent. Anita's stomach clinches with cold and prickles at the sound of her mother's voice. She knows she's doing wrong by talking to this woman. She knows she needs to get away.

She grabs Sheena's hand and dashes for the front of the tent. There stands Mom, looking at them with a raised eyebrow, but a friendly smile. "What did you girls see? A mouse or something?"

Anita doesn't realize she's panting. "No, it's just…we were being interviewed and—"

Mom leans in to look. "Oh yeah?"

Anita turns around and Sheena does, too. There was no one behind them. No one in the back of the tent. No sign of Nikki. Not even the scent of her perfume.

"Whoooa. Whoa. *Whoa*." Sheena whispers.

"You are ladies who have imaginations, huh?" Mom says, still in a happy mood. "But you filled the box, so I won't complain! I've got the tickets. Let's go eat."

۞

The food at Taste has to be bought with tickets. Anything good costs ten to twelve tickets, and drinks are always an extra five tickets. A book of tickets has twenty-five or so and, of course, you can't buy *half* a book, or just enough for what you need. The tents don't take cash because that's messy and slows things down with change-making and stuff. It all seems so complicated to Anita when she thinks about it. Working at the Channel 4 tent for a little while means earning a book of tickets, but Mom always gets more so they can have extra and take some food home. "You know we can't eat anything once we get on the train," Mom reminds them.

Of course they know. Everyone knows the stories of kids being taken off the Metro in handcuffs for eating food or chewing gum.

Mom gets the spiciest jerk chicken this side of the islands. Sheena gets the best dumplings and lo mein she is willing to stand in line for. Anita gets the yummiest curry chicken and beef patties she's ever tasted. Sheena gets a beef patty, too. Anita steals one of Sheena's dumplings. They stand in line with people of all colors and shapes, giggle with other little Black girls, listen to Mom make small talk with a Hispanic woman bouncing a baby on her hip.

When they get the food they want, they find a set of steps next to one of the imposing Federal buildings. The three of them eat while listening to a circle of beautiful men of different shades of Blackness play go-go on drums made from Hechinger's buckets. They watch people stopping and swaying or straight-up dancing to the beat. As waves of the crowd pass them, Anita seeks out anyone who could look like that Nikki woman.

"What are you thinking about?" Mom asks between bites.

Anita shrugs, her eyes focusing back on her food.

But then she feels her question and decides to ask it. "Do you think a couple of people can change the whole world? Nobody can just...change it. Can they?"

Mom turns and looks at her for a long moment. Not The Look, but a look.

"I'm just asking because, like, if there are so many things that need to be changed about the world, how do you choose just one? How do you know which one is the right one to choose?"

Mom doesn't stop looking at her. It's like she is held in place or something. Anita laughs nervously. "Sorry..."

Mom starts eating again, not saying anything. Anita does the same, feeling weird and wondering what she'd said wrong. Sheena steals some of Anita's rice. Anita takes some lo mein.

"The world needs changing. Lots of it, too. That's why I made you. With you, I have two solutions for all the world's problems," Mom says.

Sheena leans forward, bumping against Anita, her eyes wide with shock. "*I'm supposed to solve all of the world's problems?*"

Mom laughs. "No, that's not what I mean. What I mean is, I can't solve all of the world's problems myself. But I know that you two will solve one of them for me. You'll be bold and brave and get out there and do the work that must be done. You know everything you need to know to make change and do right by the world. "

Anita rolls her eyes. "But how do you *choose*? What if you're *asked*? How do you stand up and say, 'I want to change this thing more than any other thing' and know that you chose the right thing?"

Mom smiles with that same patience and warmth that Nikki had. "That's where your knowing comes in. And you know what, Anita? Sometimes, you just have to have the audacity to decide and trust your decision. Chances are, what you choose is something a whole lot of people need. More than you can possibly know."

Anita doesn't know if she wants to laugh at a joke or scream with frustration.

"We've got to get going, ladies," Mom says, stretching her legs and getting herself up.

When they get up to get rid of what they've eaten and organize what they are taking home, Mom takes a moment to assess the ticket situation. They have 13 left.

"You ladies have your Metro cards, right?" Mom asks absently, carefully putting the ticket book in her purse.

"Yes," Anita answers, a hand instinctively going to her pocket. The smooth surface therein is such an assuring feeling. Sheena yawns and stretches as she stands up. Anita's feet are starting to hurt. It is a good thing to be going back home.

It doesn't take much for them to separate from the crowd and the noise. Anita thinks that the air gets thinner and cooler not a few feet away from the tents and the party. Color and delight retreat back to the gray of the buildings. On the stairs and in the doorways, Anita's eyes go back to the faded bundles and collections of living she had noticed before.

Mom deviates from the direct walk back to the Metro station, her head turning this way and that. They've walked far enough from the crowd to be away from it, but not so far as to be out of view of it. The sounds and smells linger on their clothes and in their ears, but also echo off the buildings and down the street. Mom stops in front of a collection of things: two trash bags, a milk crate, a shopping cart, a sleeping bag. A woman, Black, with silver streaking a crown of hair that has been combed recently and put into two braids, sits on the milk crate. "You two stay right here. Do not move," Mom says.

Anita and Sheena stand there. They do not move. They watch Mom leave the sidewalk and approach the woman, who eyes her, smiling.

Mom hands her the little book of leftover tickets, placing them in the woman's hands. Anita can't hear her mother's words, but she watches her gestures—pointing toward the tents, pointing toward the ticket book. Anita can imagine the explanation: enough to get a meal. Won't be a lot, but it will be good.

The woman's lips part and form two words. Mom smiles and says two words. Then she steps away and back to the sidewalk. "Let's go, ladies."

Mom doesn't look back. She sets a purposeful pace down the sidewalk, back toward the Metro and home. Sheena runs to catch up with her. Anita walks, but looks over her shoulder to catch a glimpse at the woman. She is standing, looking at the tents.

Anita wonders what she is thinking. Her eyes sweep over to the other little groups of things and the people who live among them. She watches people with bags of food, satisfied smiles on their faces, walk by the huddled figures surrounding them without a second glance. Across the blocked off street, a single ticket skitters by, dropped and forgotten.

♋

Sheena decides to sit with Mom so she can lean on her, so Anita gets a window seat. The darkness of the tunnels below the city are uninteresting, even lulling. As much as Anita tries to find details in the darkness, all she can see is her reflection and that of her napping sister and their mom. Looking at her sister's reflection, she thinks about what Sheena already knows. She'd learned something new about her sister today. She feels a pain deep inside herself as she thinks about it.

When they emerge from the underground after Union Station, Anita stares out at the back-of-building world, grateful for the brilliance of sunlight. Among the collected things, so much debris of life, are people that Anita can see more clearly. Men, women, large and small. She can't see the finer details, but she can see them.

There are so many problems in the world. Too many to change in one ask. Anita cannot possibly know how to make it right. But when she sees Nikki again, she thinks she knows how to start.

TO THE BOTTOM

Josh Eure

THE BLACK IS EVERYWHERE AND YAWNING AS the void of space with microbe stars, one-celled critters gobbling methane and sulfur, microscopic xenophyophores absorbing their meals and sliming the sea floor—many fathoms below. Tiny crustaceans in aluminum armor drift in the white of the submersible's light like dust motes as the craft descends farther and farther into the trench.

"Nine-hundred bars," Dr. Sato says, checking the pressure gauge on her display board.

The man beside her smiles. "Barely a hug, no?"

Dr. Sato snuffles, still awed by the *Cyana*. The new submersible's impossible pressure hull design is revolutionary—a three-inch thick outer shell of titanium nanites that flex as pressures mount, allowing for dives to depths yet unknown. No longer must the hull creep steadily closer to the cabin in the dropping. Their deep suits are made with similar tech, permitting trench divers to at last leave their subs.

"You have children, Doctor?" the man asks. His name

is Dr. Charles Granger, a French biologist of some renown. He likes to talk.

Dr. Sato turns to him, noting the bizarre, eyeless fish on camera behind him. This trench has been and will continue to be a trove of new data. "We're both doctors, call me Mai. No kids, no."

"Well, count yourself lucky. I go to the bottom of the world for a little peace." The man chuckles. His beard is messy, and his hair is wet with sweat. "All my son wants to do is play video games and eat. My wife, she says I need to be stronger with him. She says he is getting strange." The man leans forward to gaze through the starboard window. "Did you see that?"

"No. What?"

"Big thing. Shark, maybe. It was moving fast."

Mai stares through the window but sees nothing. She looks down through the ventral glass at the flurry of detritus washing up and around them. Their descent is slow and measured. "Just our lights drawing attention. I'm sure the cameras got it."

"I told my son that video game players have the world's worst carbon footprint, and he just laughed at me. He is a shit."

Mai thinks of the daughter she lost, recalling the wonderful asymmetry of her smile. She grumbles to clear her throat.

The *Cyana* reaches thirty-thousand feet, a depth that was impressive just twelve years prior. But in 2031, the Japanese vessel Boijā discovered a hidden trench in the Pacific that was recorded to have a depth of 50,027 feet. Satellites revealed the emergence of the trench after a submarine earthquake weeks before its depth was confirmed, but once it was, the scientific community was electrified. Eventually the whole world was swept up in a fever to reach the bottom of Hosho Deep, so named for the robotic submersible first used to record its depth.

The groan of the hull swells as they reach thirty-one thousand feet and Mai again looks through the glass below her. She thinks of the countless pollutants that will come to litter the bottom of this trench, the reach of mankind's shoddiness almost without limit. She considers the debris in orbit above the earth as the world prepares to launch its second manned mission to Mars—just three short months from now. Mai is certain that humanity's appetite for worlds will one day be rivaled by the enormity of its leavings. But she finds it difficult to care anymore. For her, now, there is only the deep.

"What do you think it is?" Charles asks. He presses a button on his own display. "Dropping shot," he says, and dozens of round weights fall from a duct below them. Mai watches through the ventral glass as they vanish in the deep.

"The big thing you saw?"

"No, the anomaly."

Mai recalls the image from an unmanned descent last year, a blurry still of something at the bottom of Hosho Deep. There is the suggestion of illumination and the size of what is captured is considerable—an estimated fifteen feet from the right edge of the camera frame to the margins of the shape, but little else. An anomaly.

"Oh. I don't know."

Charles shakes his head. "It looks like it glows. From the picture, don't you think? Some sort of bioluminescence."

"I think the image is hard to make out," Mai says. "That's why we're here."

"Yes, yes. Explorers of the deep. Intrepid pioneers daring ever closer to the center of the Earth, yes?"

Before Mai can respond, an alarm sounds. The panel reads Failure Protocol: 16F9-43.

"Check that code," she says.

"Yes, okay. Probably one of the thrusters. The math on these pressures is going to take some trial and error."

"We're finishing this dive."

Charles looks up from the display, tilts his head. "I—yes, certainly."

After a few moments, Charles determines that the alarm was false, a problem in the wiring that Mai resolves quickly, and they continue their descent. The two of them sit in silence for an hour or more, observing occasional wildlife from the many windows around them—familiar fish and octopi, jellyfish, even a dragonfish, with its monstrous teeth and glowing lamp, its eely body wriggling in the beam of light. Down, down. So many familiar deep dwellers, but at fathoms never recorded. Textbook revisions will abound.

Conversation in the cabin, when it occurs, is banal. Mai assumes that Charles can sense her disinterest because she does little to conceal it. Finding the bottom and whatever it hides is all she cares for anymore. There are perennial protests outside NASA and her own agency's HQ, a noisy minority demanding the government stop funding space launches and descents like these. People are suffering, they shout, the cost of expeditions are astronomical, and the fossil fuels involved, the waste—these are all things Mai puts aside. Yes, people are suffering. People suffer.

Mai is in a kind of trance watching the water slide up along the port-side glass. It is the movement trails from hovering detritus seeming to draw lines up toward the surface, away from them in this four-hour long descent with little to see for much of the time save these gray, blurry lines. They almost connect when she unfocuses her eyes, and she thinks now that it is much like the inversion of a rainstorm out there—a literal shitstorm. And then everything goes black.

"What happened?" Charles says.

"The external lights are gone. Checking." Mai slides her hand along her display, swiping through dashboards until finally landing on sensors. She toggles several filters. "Bulbs are intact according to this."

"Maybe it's more electrical problems."

"Maybe. I'll pop the box for the starboard side, you check the port." Mai opens the electrical box on the wall, checks the fuses. Nothing. She investigates the wiring in the wall but finds nothing out of the ordinary.

"I cannot find," Charles says.

"Same."

They return to their seats. "We're going to have to go out there," Mai says.

"Or we return and tell the engineers to do better, because we need lights that can withstand at least sixteen-hundred bars. We are not even at the bottom yet."

"We're not scrubbing this dive, Charles."

The man hangs his head. "I don't want to either, but this is a lot of pressure and those suits—what if they fail like the lights?"

"They've been tested."

"So have the lights."

Mai rises from her seat. "Fine. I'll do it alone. You radio top-side and let them know we're deepwalking for repairs." She ambles back toward the hatch to the depressurization hold. Charles follows her.

"Jesus, Mai. I know I do not know you so well. But let me say that you seem unstable."

Mai walks into the hold and there are two deep suits affixed to the wall and floor by magnets. Their titanium nanites reflect the blue of the overhead light. She inserts her legs and leans against the wall, pushes her arms down into the sleeves.

"There is no reason for us to push this," Charles says. "There will be another chance. You know that if I radio topside and tell them we lost all external lights, they will order us to surface."

Mai grabs her gloves and helmet. She secures the harpoon pistol in the leg of her suit. "There's no guarantee we'll be chosen for the next dive. Someone else finds the anomaly and puts their name on whatever it is. Are you willing to risk that?"

"No one has ever been in a suit like this at forty-eight thousand feet. You want us to be the lab rats here?"

"I said I'll do it."

Charles rubs a hand along his scalp. "If you check every light on the sub, you will be out there some time. With the pressure. And the wildlife."

Mai dons her helmet and slides the sealing coupler closed,

releasing a hiss of heliox. She feels the internal warmers coming online. "Then by all means, Charles, stop bitching and help me."

☯

Mai engages her magboots and stands up from the port side of the outer hull, just above the ballast weights. She fastens a carabiner to one of the many mounted i-rings running the surface of the hull and checks the spool of her tether. The spotlight on her helmet reveals dozens of pale arthropods swimming around her. She steps slowly forward along the hull, aided by air jets on the back of her suit, making for the fifteen-foot light-panel. Her boot-sensors flare green with every connection, small spots of color in an otherwise black abyss.

Mai turns her head lamp toward the deep, revealing more arthropods and a massive abyssal ray, its fins undulating in a slow pitch away from her. The pressure is unbelievable, even in the deep suit. Mai feels the vibration of nanites fighting, containing the perpetual cannon blast of force. Charles was right. These suits are far from proven.

"I don't believe it is the pressure," Charles says over their local radio. He is on the starboard side of the vessel, out of sight. "The camera and light booms appear fine to me."

Mai reaches the stabilizer fin and sees that the booms on her side are also undamaged. She squats down at the upper rim of the light panel. She pulls her multitool from its pouch and uses it to unfasten the electrical hatch. The problem is immediately apparent. The power array for the lights has been overloaded. Blackened scorch marks form geographic shapes along the array beneath its vacuum case. Nodes and connections have been melted irreparably. "This array's overloaded."

"Overloaded?"

"Yes. What are you seeing?"

"I am still trying to walk to it."

Mai again gazes out into the open dark. She holds a hand up to a nearby arthropod. It floats and works its way to land on the tip of her gloved finger. The crustacean is translucent in the light.

"Yes, here too," Charles says. "Cooked."

"What could have done that?"

"Who can say? Bad wiring?"

"Let's hope not. I assume the others are out for the same reason. Let's replace these and then I'll handle the ventral panel, you take the dorsal."

"Where are the replacement arrays?" Charles asks.

"There should be a second hatch just above the one you opened."

Charles grunts into the radio. "I have it."

"And be careful not to puncture the vacuum cases. We don't want to get electrocuted."

"Aye-aye, mon capitan!"

Mai shakes her head and opens the second board, begins replacing the array. She remembers a time when work was not her life—when she put in normal hours at a lab in Woods Hole, Michigan, hiked on weekends with her husband along the Beebe and Salt Pond loops, admiring cattails in the canals at sunset with a new baby inside of her. She remembers teaching her daughter to ride a bike. Not her husband. She'd been proud of that.

Mai stands up from the electrical hatch as more than a hundred bulbs flare to life, pressing a bright white screen of light out into the water. She begins the slow trek to the ventral side of the hull. She passes over the bait station and the lifting point and down farther, careful as she ambles around the vertical and horizontal thruster ports. She finally reaches the light panel. "There it is again!" she hears over the radio.

"There what is?"

"It is fast, I cannot—"

Mai looks around in the darkness, her head lamp revealing nothing. "Charles," she says. He does not respond. "Charles?" She grabs the harpoon gun from its holster. "Charles, do you copy?"

Mai begins making her way to the dorsal side of the hull, log walking quickly up, the submersible rolling beneath her boots. As she draws nearer, she can see that Charles has managed to replace the array, a white dome of light rises like the sun as she crests over to the top of the vessel. "Charles?" She aims her pistol into the light from her head lamp, panning, finding only detritus. She works her way to the light panel and bends down to the small i-ring just beside it. Charles' carabiner is there, attached to a torn length of tether.

☙

Mai sits in her seat, gripping the glass display of her command board. She has managed to slow her breathing, to push panic from her mind only a little, and she swipes to access the comm dashboard. She presses the button for voice transmission. "Surface, this is *Cyana*."

"Go ahead, *Cyana*."

Mai closes her eyes. Charles is gone. "Go ahead, *Cyana*. Over." She waited for him to return, resisting the urge to pilot the sub away from their stopping point to see if she could locate him. The vastness of this canyon means that it was better for her to remain, to allow *Cyana's* lights to guide Charles back from the abyss. If the creature he'd seen before was a predator— "*Cyana*, do you copy? Over." She swam around in the darkness tethered to the hull for an hour, risking whatever it was that took him—if something took him—she shouted over their radio and he never responded.

"We copy, surface," Mai says. "Standby. Over."

"Copy that."

Mai feels the symptoms of shock still, though less after vomiting in the depressurization hold. She feels outside of her body now, spying herself through the dorsal glass leaning forward in her seat, holding her head, no, a man has died in this lonesome place because of her, because of her. She could have scrubbed the dive. There is no knowing what lives in these depths. The suits are for emergencies, Charles knew, she knew. For escaping a hull breach or life support systems failure, not for blown lights. The replacement parts are there for quick fixes before launch, not at minus forty-eight thousand feet. But even so, from her position, observing herself from without this way, she sees the decision coming as she sits upright and presses the comm button once more, hears herself speak. "Surface, we had a hiccup, but we're continuing descent. Will contact on landing. Over."

"Copy, *Cyana*."

The decision to go to the bottom is out of Mai's hands. She decided long ago. All she can do now is watch herself going down, down, down.

☯

The *Cyana* touches down on the sea floor and Mai radios the surface to confirm a successful landing. She ignores the congratulations, declaring that she is at this moment maneuvering the *Cyana* toward the location of the anomaly. The external lights reveal a barren and lunar landscape, rocks and sand pillowing up from the seabed as the horizontal thrusters propel the Cyana forward. Fish flitter out of the submersible's path and Mai checks all windows and cameras. She sees nothing but the suspended emptiness of a desolate world hiding untold creatures. She sees the void where she has come in search of phantasms and where a man was lost in her coming, and yet still she persists—down, all the way. Searching, thinking of nothing else. Hunting.

And there it is. There. A blue bright eye, bioluminescent and blinking from behind the canyon wall. A black line pupil. An eye. A single, glowing eye.

Mai scans the wall to find a point of entry, some hole large enough for the *Cyana* to fit through but finds nothing. If the size of the eye is an indicator, the creature is gargantuan and so must have found itself on the other side of the wall by descending from somewhere far above. Was this what took Charles?

Mai peers through the dorsal glass, using a small joystick to drag the spotlight up the canyon wall, but spies no end. She looks back to the hole, to the eye—strangely intelligent how it blinks.

"Surface, this is *Cyana*. Be advised, I'm near the southwestern wall of the canyon and the anomaly is on the other side. There are no points of entry to whatever recess is beyond that will fit the submersible. So I'm deepwalking. Over."

Mai does not wait for confirmation before removing her headset and making for the depressurization hold. She presses the pneumatic release and opens the hatch. She removes her deep suit's magboots and replaces them with heavy diving fins then dons the suit, seals her helmet. She presses the switch for depressurization and water induction. She waits for the pressure to normalize, ignoring all thoughts of safety in this alien place. She thinks only of the eye, the brilliant blue-white eye larger than the sub. As the pressure equalizes, water begins to flood into the hold from an induction port on the titanium floor. Seawater roils and foams as it slowly fills the room. The water line sloshes up against Mai's helmet glass before finally reaching the ceiling. The hatch on the far end of the hold opens.

Mai emerges into free water, kicks her diving fins up toward the space in the wall where she'd seen the eye. The side of this canyon is stippled by milky anemones, which flower open and closed in her passing. She grips her harpoon gun in one hand, swimming close to the wall, glancing around and behind her. As she reaches the craggy gap, she slows. She flutters her fins to reverse as she rises, but as she reaches the level of the opening, she sees that the eye is gone. She looks around again then shines her light into the hole once more.

The eye returns.

Mai panics and fires a harpoon, but misses. It clatters harmlessly against the canyon wall. And somehow, Mai feels compelled to go to the eye. In her mind she hears a calling come, come. So, she goes.

☲

The great beast stoops, bringing its goblinish face farther down, closer. A creature of immense size, strangely ambulatory and hulking like a thing from land in the shadow of the canyon wall. The bioluminescence of its skin markings and its eyes are bright enough to allow Mai to see it without her headlamp, so she clicks it off. There is another beast here that does not move, simply watches from its place behind the first. Mai trembles at the sight of them where she is, weightless in the deep, the extreme pressure against her suit causing nanites to shutter and grind, signaling they can take little more.

"Do not struggle, little ape."

Mai blinks, certain she heard the words in her mind. They boomed and reverberated. They blew a speaker in her skull.

"The words come to you as meager as your own biology. They sound like deflating squids because your mind lacks the pliancy. It is enough that you understand. We can move forward." The beast looks back toward the other beast. "Why do you argue when you know how it goes? And there I go. Arguing against you when I know you will argue and I will ignore you and you will be drawn in and this whole thing will go as it goes, blah, blah, blah. Yes. Yes. I love you down and down to the very bottom, yes."

Mai touches the front of her pressure suit, feeling the constriction on her chest. She checks the display on her wrist—1,533.74 bars.

"Your calculations and trinkets have brought you far. You can speak to me now, if you like. You've come all this way."

Mai is unsure how to do so. Can the creature hear her thoughts, should she—

"Yes, yes. Speak out loud, for your sake. Use your vibrating slug of a throat for its purpose and we can get on with all of this." The creature returns its attention to the other. "Yes, of course. I know."

"What are you?" Mai asks.

"What am I?" the creature says, his great eyes closing. "Did you hear that, love? The little ape asks what we are. Yes, of course,

I know. Still." The creature rests on its haunches now, causing a swell of sediment to blossom up from the seafloor. "I am what you see. The very thing before you, what else? What do you think I am?"

Mai shakes her head. "I…we have never seen a creature like you. Nothing that can do what apparently you can."

"You think I am goblinish."

"No—"

"No?" the creature says. "Did you hear that, love?"

"I'm sorry," Mai says. "Your features, they're unfamiliar to me, is all. They look—"

"Yes, yes. I know too much and this is tedious now. Say what you came to say."

Mai frowns. "We came to explore. I didn't come to say anything. I didn't know a thing like you—"

"You know that is untrue and I know it also. The moment I touched your mind and you realized our magnitude you had a question for me. And I mean for you to ask it. You are also afraid for your friend who vanished, correct?"

Mai flutters her diving fins in a way to keep herself facing the creature.

"Let me soothe you at least in that regard," the creature says. "My love here took him. She ushered him back home."

Mai sputters, fogging her helmet glass.

"No," the creature says. "He is safe above, from whence you came. He will have no understanding of what happened to him."

"How?"

"Please. Ask your question."

"Was it you that damaged our lights?"

The creature wrinkles up its nose. "Of course not. There are some down here with lightning of their own. It was one of these which halted you. It intended to harm your friend as well, but my love sent it on its way."

Mai looks up toward the surface, relieved that Charles is alive and safe. "You claim to have answers for me," she says. "How?

You hide in the deepest part of the ocean on Earth. How can you know of anything beyond this trench?"

"Not the deepest. Merely the deepest in this moment. But yes. I know because whatever you name that which conjured this time-stricken reality sees fit for me to know. My love and I are not limited to remembrance and perception only. We see too what *will* be. Even now, we see it."

"The future?"

"Yes."

"How is that possible?"

"Because it is. Therefore, it is."

Mai pulls her knees up toward her chest, positioning herself to see better. "You know how the world ends?"

The creature nods. "Of course. *This* world, yes."

"It's us, isn't it? Humans?"

"That is not the question you are here to ask."

"I'm asking it. Therefore, it is."

The creature turns again to the other of its kind. "You must help me. I cannot bear it. This is so very long-winded."

The other lowers its head and appears to sleep.

"Yes, exactly. Of course." The creature returns its attention to Mai. "All right. Please do not interrupt, even though you will, blah, blah, blah, and so on." The creature leans forward, widening its bioluminescent eyes. "We are very old and we are very few. We do not require much to sustain ourselves. Our size and dimensions and features have nothing to do with your evolutionary mandates or with our environs. So, everything you've learned about this world and its creatures will be of no use to you. That is fine for our purposes."

"How can—"

"An interruption. The first of three. Let us move on."

Mai chews at her bottom lip, awash with questions she can feel the creature ignoring in her mind. What use are its toes and the width of its nostrils, the nodules running the length of its skin? How does its body resist the pressure? What must it eat and how often to achieve such immense size, and what does that mean for abyssal gigantism? Why—

"We have seen the beginning of life on Earth as well as its end. We can see them both now and we will continue to do so until our end. This is not important. Neither is the why of our kind. We simply are and we do.

"You and many of your kind believe you will be the cause of the Earth's destruction. This is true. You are ending life on Earth as we speak. But the way I am forced to speak to you of this is clutched by time as a principle. This is a hindrance, as you can imagine."

"Wait—"

"That is two. I will permit you this diversion. Go on."

Mai inhales. "We destroy all life on Earth? You know this?"

The creature raises what might be an eyebrow. "Indeed."

"Then why go on? Why talk to me or do anything? Why participate in something so futile?"

"Look where we are. This is as close to us not participating as we can muster. No, no. Now I am simply being goblinish. In truth, I answered that before you interrupted. And I knew you would miss it. And now here we are."

"Right. Blah, blah, blah."

"Indeed. The whys of us are not important, little ape. We are and we do. May I?"

Mai nods, feeling the start of a headache.

"Time is what gives you your sense of tragedy for the world's end. I see beyond time. If I do not enjoy the end, I will return to the beginning. Or I may focus entirely on the middle. But none of that is accurate because the notion of beginnings and middles and ends is born from time—is intrinsically bound by it. Do you see the problem?"

"I do."

"Good, yes. Well, the other thing is that this end of all life is not a fixed point. It is not an absolute. It is only one of countless others. We see the others as well. Let us call them pins—ends, middles, moments, memories, possibilities. They are pins. The one in charge of the pins—call it God or some simulacrum—is quite fickle but, above all, desires and glories in free will. And so, while it might have the power to move the pins or arrange them in a given way, it prefers not to. Until it does not. As I said, fickle. There is an overall plan, mind you. The earthquake that uncovered our home, say, which drew you to us. If one were made to suppose a motive—perhaps to keep things interesting. Or not. Nothing so simple, surely. Nevertheless, these pins are created in their multitudes and arrayed against the many life-forms of this world and other worlds and chained to you all by time. But the funny thing is, all of you create the pins. Free will and everything that goes with it."

"I'll use my third interruption now."

"Of course, you will."

"This makes no sense."

The creature raises a knobbed hand to its torso. Mai notices a thumb. "Of course," it says.

"Will you stop that? You may know everything, but I'm trying here."

"Yes. Well, you must understand all that I know and all that I observe of existence as you struggle to speak in this moment—it is no small task."

"Then why put up with it? Why not check out?"

"Because it is not what we do. Please. Continue."

Mai puts a hand on her helmet. Her headache worsens with every word the creature imparts. "Forgetting the nonsense of pins, if there are countless endings, why do you see the end of all life on Earth? Why don't you say you see how humanity creates a utopia that goes on forever? Or a future where flowers take over the world?"

"Because you asked if I saw humans destroying this world. I do."

"But you see the others as well? Life continuing forever?"

"What is forever without time? A word without meaning."

Mai shuts her eyes, a familiar agony beginning to bloom. The weeks in the hospital with her daughter and the weeks after her daughter died, Mai wanted to peel the skin from her own arms, the muscles. She wanted access to the bone. And Mai's attempts to wrangle it now are like flapping in a free-fall. Her guts are hauled upward, and she fights to keep from vomiting in her helmet. She takes big gulps of heliox. She checks her gauge—less than ten percent left. Her helmet glass drips condensation.

"Be at peace, little ape."

"My name is Mai! I'm a human being! And I don't believe any of this! Because this is interruption number *four*!"

"No."

"No? What do you mean no?"

"This is not an interruption. Finally, at last. This is the point. Ask what you came to ask."

Mai bends at the waist and begins to cry. She rolls in the black water, coughing, sobbing. She thinks of her daughter in the grass on her first day of school, posing for a picture by the flower bed. Her black hair in a ponytail. And without fail, the memory of her daughter without that hair comes like a riptide, and the size of the coffin and her husband begging for attention and affection only months after she was gone—how dare he? How could he? Mai shudders, the grip of it all drawing her down, paralyzing her in the deep before these preternatural creatures where they dare to suppose they have answers.

"How dare you?"

"Yes."

"How could you?"

"Of course."

She waits. She will not ask it because the creature already knows.

"Mai Sato," the creature says. "You pretend that you do not know, but you do know. This answer is nothing new to you. And it will not satisfy, but it is true. Free will is never without consequence. Time is never without end. You will know peace."

"How can I? I don't want to live in this world without her."

"You understand now. This will pass as time always demands. Endure, go on."

"No. That's not an answer. That's a platitude. You'll get through it, stay strong, blah, blah, blah. Why does God or the big alien or builder of this simulation allow suffering? Why? Why allow an innocent life to be taken? Why the disease and the hunger and the shit? Why?"

"Why was your daughter taken from you?" The question is communicated through Mai's mind, but she can somehow tell that it comes from the creature's mate, which has suddenly raised its head.

"Yes!" Mai says. "Yes, why? Why?"

"Of course. This, you will never understand. You are not meant to."

"No, I'm asking you why?"

"We have always known that you would bring this grief to us down here, and yet we did not flee. We did not abandon you, though we knew you could never understand. You ask the wrong questions and are confused by the right answers."

Mai struggles to breathe and looks at her heliox gauge again—two percent. Her headache has become a living thing. "Will I ever see her again?"

"Of course, you will. You already have."

"When? How?"

The other creature rises now and ambles slowly to stand before Mai. Its legs are bent trees covered by toady, dark skin. It blinks. "You will return to your vessel because if you do not, you will die. You do not want to die, and you will not. You have learned of us and so we will leave and find a new home. You feel you did not get the answer you wanted and that is both true and false. You feel grateful to us for endeavoring to help you when we have no obligation to, but that is not true. Because this is what we do. You will not tell of your encounter with us because it is not what you do, and we thank you for that. There will be consequences for your unwavering descent here, but you will be redeemed. You will continue to dive in this trench, and you will discover many new life forms. But you will never see our like again. You will slowly heal, but only a little, and your daily work will satisfy. You will love again on this Earth, but never as before. One day, the world will learn of us and that is fine. Because on that day, all life will be free from time. And you will all know the peace we enjoy. But it is not now. Go."

Mai looks down at her heliox levels and confirms that the creature is right. She has no time left. And she has a thought to remain, to let the deep claim her and make a liar of these wondrous beings. To let the torment of a life without her child die away in the abyss. To feel that blissful erasure of consciousness. But that is not what she does.

Mai turns and begins the short trip back to the *Cyana*. She can just hear the hiss of the air jets over the pounding of her headache. She reaches the depressurization hold and closes the hatch. She slams her glove against the ejection plate and the waterline drops steadily to the floor. She breathes the last remaining heliox in her tank as the pressure normalizes and she opens the hatch to the cabin and falls through.

Mai removes her helmet. "I'll see her again?" she says, gasping.

"You have," Mai hears in her mind. "You will."

SHOCK OF BIRTH

CADWELL TURNBULL

"**T**HEY DIDN'T BELIEVE ME," I SAID. "THEY didn't believe that I wasn't supposed to be here—that I woke up wrong."

I lost track of time again. My attention shifted towards the floor, drawn to a crack in the tile. It was causing quite a ruckus in my mind. The cup of tea I was holding had long gone cold, the light in the room growing dim.

Once, a long time ago, someone dropped something heavy on the tile and it was never the same.

"What does it mean to wake up wrong?" Sarah pressed. I could feel her breath on me, circling me, touching my skin. I could feel my fingers against the porcelain of the mug. The sun was setting and I could feel my eyes adjust to the changing light. Only this skin, these fingers, these eyes—they weren't mine. No one ever understood when I told them. They always gave me the same look, wide eyes, open mouth.

"I woke up in the wrong place," I said. "I was somewhere else, some other life somewhere and then I was here, in this life. The bed I woke up in was wrong. My room. My age. My parents. They didn't like being told that they were wrong. My teacher didn't like it. The kids at school."

Wide eyes. Open mouth.

"They want me to lie. And I won't."

The lights in the room came on. I wondered how long it took shuffling through dark rooms before people started putting suns in their houses, before they stopped depending on the one outside.

"Australia is gone," Sarah said. "Now there's only ocean there. No one believes me."

I got up; I did it so fast my head felt light and for a minute I was wobbly. I held onto the back of the chair to get my bearings. "I'm going to my room," I said.

Sarah watched me. I had hurt her somehow. I felt a pang of guilt, but didn't act on it. As I walked out the room I remembered that I had left my mug on the table. I was supposed to put it in the kitchen, but my pride stopped me from going back.

❡

There weren't many cars on the freeway. Orange and yellow painted the early morning horizon, edging against the black. The eyes of the world were opening: yellow and orange twisting around dark colored clouds along the horizon, slowly claiming the still black sky above, the sleeping people below in their houses, just starting to wake to their busy days, their lives waiting just a few hours ahead of coffee and toast.

Michael slept in the back, huddled up in his usual position. Every once in a while, his whole body would twitch and then he'd turn in the opposite direction. He did this dance for the last four hours, facing away from me, and then toward me again. Right now I could see his face, underneath his mass of curls. He seemed peaceful; a few hours ago he was yelling obscenities at me and trying to hit me with his clenched fist. I had to tie his hands behind his back.

Michael had a nervous habit of playing with the sleeves of his shirt or working the tail of his watch in and out of its loop as he talked, head lowered only when he was saying something that he felt was too aggressive. Even when he cursed he would only look at me for a second before whipping his head away.

His choice of clothing was similar to what I remembered. He wore his pants baggy but his shirts were tight around his bony frame and wide chest; his sleeves were loose around his thin wiry arms. His pants were ripped at the bottom from dragging; they were too big for him and he often stopped mid-step to fold it up one or two times so the denim wouldn't catch under his shoe.

He was twenty now, a college student. Half what I was when I'd been pulled out of my body, half what I was now. In the morning half-light, his dark skin appeared darker. This skin that wasn't mine appeared very pale in comparison.

"What do you want?" he asked.

☯

"No," I said.

Dr. Stevens seemed genuinely surprised by my response. His face was usually stolid when he talked and asked questions. BBut every once in a while, if only for a moment, a response lets itself loose, from his brain to his face muscles, revealing genuine emotion.

"I never said I didn't know them," I said.

"Yes, but you did say they were wrong. Did you mean that you felt that they weren't your parents?"

"No. I never said they weren't my parents. You don't listen."

"Elaborate," he said. "Explain it to me now."

"I said they were the wrong parents."

"Yes?" His face was blank this time. It would be a while before another emotion was clever enough to escape, a while before another one would be shot and dragged to the back of his mind where he left the bodies. I looked at his wall of books. Thick books with leather spines. Hardcover books with golden type on the sides. They were all related to psychology, except for one, hiding in the corner, thin and worn. A paperback. Anne Rice. *The Vampire LeStat.*

He was watching me and playing with his white beard streaked with black. I tried to picture him at a time when his hair still had his color, but no matter how many wrinkles I took away from his face, I could not change his hair. It was always white with black streaks, wild and bushy.

"They were wrong because I was wrong. They're Daniels' parents, but I am not Daniel. I am supposed to be someone else."

"Who are you supposed to be?" he asked. He was staring at me, a blank canvas to be painted on.

"You won't believe me."

"Just tell me what you believe."

"I'm Michael. I was stitched into this life."

"That is a very interesting word: 'stitched.' Please continue."

"I went to sleep. I had a nightmare. And when I woke up, I was in the wrong place. It was the wrong year, the wrong city, the wrong house, the wrong bedroom. I came back to the wrong body. And now I am trapped here with you, answering your questions, watching you scribble in your pad. I am here, wondering what combination of words would make a sane man believe me. And I am here, knowing, that even if you did, even if you abandoned your sanity and believed every single word, you still couldn't help me get back. And it would be a waste. It would all be a waste."

For a moment I thought I could see Dr. Steven's hands shake. "You are quite a precocious child."

"I am not a child."

"You know what we do at this institute?"

"I do."

"We study people that think the world has been edited. There's someone here that believes there's more than fifty states in the U.S. and one of them got erased. There's a girl that swears there's an entire continent missing, and an adult man that believes his sister didn't exist before this year."

"I'm not like them."

"Really? If you're here, who is in Michael's body?"

"I don't know yet. He hasn't been born."

"And you don't find that convenient? Where will he be born?"

I looked up at his eyes and saw the truth written plainly there. I could tell him the future I knew, but what if that future didn't come? I glanced back over at his bookshelf and looked at the little book in the corner again, pressed hard against the shelf wall, sandwiched in by books and wood, kept in place by the laws of matter. As incongruous as it was, it was still a book. Still binding and paper.

"Where?" he asked again.

♋

When I didn't answer right away Michael huffed and kicked the back of the passenger's seat. It was mid-afternoon now, which meant winding backroads with only two lanes to avoid being seen. This particular stretch of road was empty, long periods with no cars, the bare hills merging with blue sky.

"Northern California," I said.

"Why are we going to North California?"

I'd watched Michael long enough to know he was different. It was little things. Like how he chose to wear his hair. I always kept mine cut. His teeth weren't as healthy as mine. He seemed to worry less about what he wore than I did.

His grades were lower but not much lower than mine when I was his age. His friends were the same for the most part, with a few exceptions. He had grown into a subtly different person, and he had conversations with people I never did and liked people I never liked. But it was the eyes that really separated us. If I stared at them long enough, I could see that he wasn't me, that some other person was living behind them. Same face, different insides.

"Don't worry," I said. "I have no intention of harming you."

He said nothing and I wondered if he could see into me the same way, sense my insides. It should go both ways, a thing like that.

C♂

"Shock of birth," I said.

The building was colder than usual. Dr. Steven rubbed his hands together to warm them and it sounded like sandpaper against wood. The furrows in his brow told me that he was actually interested.

I said, "In Nepal, the elders tell the children that the soft spot in a baby's head is from God's hammer, to make the baby forget its past life. For Plato, it was the act of entering the body that made a person forget. The shock of birth."

Dr. Stevens was rubbing his hands together again and this time it reminded me of a childhood memory. My mother bent over, sweeping the floor with a broom with a broken handle. Dried sorghum bristles against ceramic tile. As I listened, it occurred to me that there were so many things that sounded similar. The thought unnerved me.

"I didn't enter this body from birth. I was thrust into it in its adolescence. And so I retained all my memories."

Dr. Stevens rubbed his hands together. Sandpaper. Bristles. Folders in filing cabinets. "So how do you explain that?"

"Pythagoras had another theory about reincarnation. He believed that there was a river. The souls would bathe in that river before entering another body. The 'river of forgetfulness' it was called. This was an agreement, a law among spirits."

"Okay," Dr. Stevens said. "Seems like a complicated explanation, when a simple one would do." He let the implication hang between us. You're delusional, he was saying, but didn't have the courage to say out loud. He looked up at the clock. "That's time for today. I should go see what's going on with the heating system."

As I was walking back to my room, I saw Sarah standing by my door. "I talked to Jacob from down the hall and he said that he was the one that told Dr. Stevens that a state was missing."

"Oh," I said, but I was distracted.

"Yeah," she continued. "Only he said that in his timeline—that's how he said it, his 'timeline'—there were also only fifty states, but one of them was Alaska."

"Alaska," I said, repeating the word. It sounded made up.

I opened my door and went inside. Sarah followed me in. "He said that it was actually two edits, not one. Alaska and the Californias."

I picked up the quilt from on the bed and wrapped it around myself. "Aren't you cold?" I asked.

She shook her head. "Not really. But I know what's wrong."

"What's wrong?"

She walked over and sat on the bed. "October's missing this year and the heating system hasn't caught up yet."

I sat next to her on the bed. "There is a question somewhere in the back of my head that I want to ask you, but I don't know what it is."

"I wish I could find it for you," she said with a half-smile. "It is strange that there is a whole world behind people's eyes that you don't get to see."

"It is. But I wonder if you would be able to find it in the back of my head. I am having trouble myself."

"Have you seen your parents lately?"

"Yesterday."

"What did they talk to you about?"

"The same thing they always talk to me about. Have I given up on this ridiculous story? Am I ready to come home? So on. So on."

Sarah had a habit of biting her bottom lip. It was a completely asexual process, like the way some people crack their knuckles. "What were you just thinking?" she asked.

"I think they're right. I should have kept quiet."

"You know, I believe you." She was silent for a moment, biting her bottom lip. "If you find the other Michael, what will you do?"

"He isn't Michael."

"I was thinking, wouldn't it be better to just live this life. If he is born in your body, that wouldn't be his fault. The rest of us have to live with what's missing. You should try living as who you are now."

"Of course you'd think that," I said. "You're insane." I immediately regretted it as soon as I said it. Over the months, I had made it my personal mission to upset Sarah. I didn't want to, but I felt a pull towards hostility.

The hurt on her face made my stomach hurt. "There's a whole continent missing, Michael. People, animals, plants. You're not so special that you can step on everyone." Then she left and we didn't talk again for twenty-five years.

☯

Time is sneaky. When you are not looking, it runs away from you. When you find it again, you are so far from where you were.

Storm clouds had settled over the desert landscape. It wasn't raining, but the promise was there. Michael was quiet in the back seat, but I could hear his breathing over the engine of the car, the sound of the wheels gliding against the tar beneath it, over the sound of the wind that continued to hit against the windows. It was making quite a ruckus in my mind.

When the car started to slow, he noticed. "What's happening?"

I didn't answer. Instead I turned the steering wheel towards the desert, towards the stretching nothingness, towards the man I used to be. The brakes screeched, the wheels spitting up gravel. The turn had pushed him up against the window, and he let out a grunt before he took in a sharp breath, a harsh thing that whistled through his teeth. I could hear him clearly; I was so tuned to his every response, like the volume was turned up on him alone.

I continued to drive until I hit a rock or a lump of dirt and the car stopped. I pulled up the handbrake and opened the door. My own breath was wild and hard, and I could feel my chest swell and sink like the belly of a giant. When I opened the backseat door and I reached in to pull at the boy's collar, he let out a noise of comprehension. He screamed out but it was not my voice. It was the voice of a stranger.

I threw him into the dirt. I was surprised by my own calm, how the rage bubbled deep in me. He looked up at me, delirious and confused. His hands were still behind his back, so he pulled himself along, backwards, his legs kicking up dust and gravel.

"Who are you?" I stepped forward towards him as he tried to scurry across the parched earth. The setting sun and the storm clouds cast everything in shadow, but I could still see his eyes, sparkling with a sheen of tears.

"I don't know what you're talking about," he said. "I don't know what this is." His mouth opened to say something more, but then he just shook his head. "Please," he begged, "I just want to go home."

"You're lying." The mouth I was using was dry, the bubble in me coming to a boil. "You took my body. You took my life. I'm going to take it back."

"What?"

"Do you know what it is like to have everything stolen from you without knowing why? I've been trapped here, in this body. Do you know I had someone I loved?"

There were many names for it. The hammer of God. The shock of birth. Drinking from the river of forgetting. It all meant the same thing. When a soul re-entered a body, it could not keep all the memories of where and who it was before. You had to give up something. You had to give up everything you once were.

He was shaking his head again. "If you let me go, I won't tell anyone. I swear."

I couldn't see his face then. It was obscured by his hair, the storm clouds, and the coming dark. But the fork was there in front of me just the same, the potential to walk this all back or take it to the bitter end.

"Please," he said. "I swear."

He seemed to be holding his breath as I decided. There was no sound but the wind. "Okay," I said and took a step forward. "Let me help you up."

☙

Moments later the storm clouds departed, so sudden that the setting sun that replaced it collected on the surface of the world like a light from heaven, painting everything with the vibrant orange of stoked embers.

It was beautiful to see it as it happened, to see the world change.

○

After many years I finally tracked down Sarah. She was on the top floor of an old apartment building on York Island. She recognized me right away. Her apartment was small, her dining table only inches from her stove. She moved on her small feet the way I remembered and went to the fridge and pulled out a pitcher of water. She grabbed two cups from her cabinet, returned to the table and sat across from me.

"It's been so long," she said. "You've changed a lot since I last saw you. But you also haven't changed at all." She was smiling. She was still so beautiful.

"How have you been?"

"I got better if that's what you're asking. It was really bad for a while, when I was in college, but I've been taking medicine. Dr. Stevens died a few years back, you know? He was always wondering where you went off to."

"You still notice edits?" I asked, looking into her almond eyes.

"Don't keep track anymore." She eased back in her chair, sighed. "Most of the time I forget what I've noticed." She poured me a cup of water and slid it over to me. Then she poured herself a cup. She put her hair back into a ponytail and took a sip of her water. "People take for granted that the world works the way it does. No one walks and questions the steps they take. They never think: 'This floor might not be solid; I could take this step and fall to the center of the earth.' No one worries that one day gravity will be reversed and everyone will helplessly fall into outer space. I've been trying to learn from them. Trust everything, even if my memory tells me differently. When people tell me there's always been only ten months in the year, I don't even blink."

I nodded. "Smart."

"And you?" she asked. "Did you ever go find yourself?" she asked.

"No," I said.

"No?"

"A couple years ago the town I lived in disappeared. The people are gone." It was the truth, however convenient.

"I suppose all our stories end that way," she said, true sympathy on her face.

"I was terrible back then."

"You were," she said. "I forgave you a long time ago. For my sake."

I nodded. "I'm still sorry," I said. "And I'm grateful to be forgiven, no matter the why." We drank our water in a companionable silence. We were both so much older now, but the years had been kinder to her. I hadn't been able to settle down anywhere and it showed in all the small ways a body and soul deteriorates without roots. I considered the possibility of settling now, and for the first time in a long time, I liked the thought of it. "You know," I said, "I've been looking at the edits a different way lately. And it has helped me."

She asked me to explain and so I did. I said it wasn't the world that was changing: it was us. We were moving, leap-frogging from universe to universe, each one different than the one before, with less stuff in it, or different stuff. We remember what we can of those other worlds, and we forget too. But here's the important part, the part that has been helping me lately. Every new world we enter gives us an opportunity to be different, to leave parts of ourselves behind, to be better. It is okay to want that, to let some things go. A body is just a body, a world is just a world, but who we are now, on the inside, is what matters. It matters. We can let go to make space for who we can become.

"That's beautiful," she said and I could see in her eyes that she meant it.

I NOT I

M. Darusha Wehm

"**I** DON'T BELONG HERE."

Marko frowns and it smashes into me again. I'm hanging out with Marko García. *The* Marko García, whose face is on the cover of Stagecraft Magazine, whose name is on top of the holomarquee at The Roxy, where the lineup for tickets runs around the corner every day. It was ridiculous enough to get to act with him, even if it was just as a local extra and my only line was, "Yes, Your Honour." But what the hell am I doing in his hotel room at one in the morning, drinking whisky and shooting the shit?

"You do, Immy," he says, the frown morphing into a smile. "I'm famous and you aren't yet, but that doesn't mean we can't be friends. I hope." His face takes on a look of mild panic and I can't help but laugh. He might not be the greatest actor of my generation, but the millions of rabid fans worldwide aren't nothing. Any one of them would literally murder me to take my place right now, and Marko is worried that *I'm* going to ghost *him*.

"I noticed that 'yet,'" I say, grinning. "Now you're just flattering me."

He arches an eyebrow and says, "You deserve to be famous if that's what you want. But it's not all it's cracked up to be." He picks up the bottle, making a gesture toward my empty glass and I nod. He pours expertly.

"How long has it been since you had to sling drinks to make rent?" I ask.

"A few years," he admits. "But when was the last time you had to sneak into a hotel using the staff entrance to avoid the media drones?"

I know what he's saying, and he's right. Still, I can't help myself, and I stage-gesture staring at the middle distance between us, up and to the right, as if focusing on the clock projected by my lenses.

"About two and a half hours ago."

"And imagine that's your everyday life, 24/7, 365?"

"Fair enough," I say, taking a slug of the whisky and standing. "Mind if I open a window? They must have the heat on for winter already. It's getting a little warm in here."

ㅇ

"I don't deserve this."

Thérèse tilts her head in that way she does when she's trying not to tell me I'm an idiot. "I don't know whether you mean the champagne or the promotion, but either way you're wrong."

I click my glass against hers, a flash of memory from our wedding nearly twenty years ago lighting up my mind. "I'm just worried I'm not up to it—running the entire Oceania branch. What if I ruin everything? All those people counting on us for aid, for expertise. What if I run the organization into the ground?"

"Shh," Thérèse says, laying her hand on mine. "You're going to be brilliant. It's good that you care, that's what makes you right for this job. I know you can do it. Imogen, this is everything you've worked for, everything you've trained for, all these years. You're going to make a fantastic Executive Director." She leans in toward me, kissing me lightly but intently.

"Okay," I say when she finally pulls away. "You're the smartest person I know, and if you think I can do it, I probably can."

"That's what I'm talking about!" She lifts the bottle of champagne and refills my glass. I get up, go to the french doors and look out into our garden. Now that the kids have gone, I can't even remember the last time I spent any time out there. I slide open the doors and a warm breeze hits my face.

"Come on, let's sit outside. It's almost summer."

☯

I'm wiping down the last few tables; my feet are sore and my back aches. Tomorrow's rehearsal doesn't start until noon, so I can sleep in if my roommate doesn't wake me up getting ready for her office job.

"I'm going to head out, Immy," Ellis, the bartender, says. We are the last two staff left, but I nod. It's a quiet Wednesday and the first really cold night of winter, and there's no one in the bar. Fifteen minutes and I should be out of here, too. My smartring vibes and I blink my lenses to life to see a text from Marko. His tour must have reached Montréal by now. I flick my eye to open it.

It's a photo, a selfie of him in bed. Just his face, looking sleepy. Tan skin made darker by a hotel room's low light, those brown eyes I could stare at for centuries. The web of wrinkles at their edges from his smile. That dimple. That fucking beautiful dimple.

"I miss your face xx," the caption reads. I go behind the bar to the mirrored wall where the liquor bottles stand in formation. I look like shit. My face is greasy, my eyeliner is smeared and my dye job needs a refresh. The blues are starting to fade toward green.

I run my fingers under my eyes to fix the makeup and swipe a cocktail napkin over my forehead and nose. I undo my braid and finger comb my long hair. Good enough. I flick my eyes in the pattern that opens my camera app and snap a few selfies. I scroll through, pick the cutest one and pump up the blues with a filter. Click send, then send another text.

"I miss your everything."

☯

My Fitbit's alarm goes off, waking me to the low light of morning. I was dreaming again. I can't remember it, the details. Only the shape of a name—Mark or Mario—and the desire. Hot, urgent, still pulsing through my body. I try to remember the face, what he looks like, this literal man of my dreams, but it's indistinct, like the faded memory of a description. I try to picture the rest, the scenario, but it's just as vague. Was it a café? A restaurant? Why was I there?

Thérèse rolls over, my movements waking her, and she nuzzles her nose into my neck. I wriggle around to pull her into my arms, my lips finding hers.

"Good morning, indeed," she says a few minutes later. "Are we going to be late for work?"

I laugh, my voice low. "That's one of the upsides about being in charge, isn't it?"

"I'll show you who's in charge." She grabs my wrists and kisses me hard.

I realize in the shower that I didn't think of him at all when we made love. That makes me feel better, but somehow also a little bit guilty, which makes me feel guilty in an entirely different way.

What the hell is wrong with me?

☯

"How was work?" Ellis asks as I dump my backpack in the office.

"Don't ask," I groan. "Rehearsal was terrible. I forgot half my blocking and stepped on Damon's foot when he made his entrance in Act II and that was probably the least of my incompetence. This is the biggest break of my entire acting career and I'm blowing it."

"Well, that's the point of rehearsal, right?" They pour three glasses of wine and add them to the highball on the counter, and I load up my tray.

"Sure, but we're supposed to be getting better as we get closer to opening," I say, taking the drinks to the table of customers engrossed in the ballet on the holo. When I get back to the bar, Ellis is looking at me oddly.

"What?" I ask. "Something on my face?"

They shake their head, their uproar of black and white curls dancing around their angular face. "Just wondering if anything's going on. You know, if something happened, that's why you're off your game?"

I give them a quizzical look. "Naw, just sleep troubles," I shrug. "No big deal."

It's accurate but not entirely true, both the excuse and my nonchalance. I'd slept like a log for eight hours. It was that stupid dream.

I'm used to having sex dreams, especially with whatever this long-distance thing with Marko is turning into, but not sweet domestic lesbian sex dreams. I can't remember any of the details, can't picture anything about her now—this literal woman of my dreams—but I know I loved her. Like, rest-of-my-life kind of love, and I haven't been able to shake that feeling all day. Every time I think I'm over it, it sneaks up on me like a stalker. A wave of warmth comes over me, as if someone slipped me some new low-key party drug.

You'd think that would feel nice, but it doesn't. It's not me who loves this woman.

But it is me. Some other me.

A large, rowdy party comes into the bar and for once I'm glad for the rush. It's a busy Friday night with the ballet and a new opera on the holos, and I manage not to think about much beyond drinks and food orders for a few hours.

I catch Ellis staring at me a couple of times, as if they're monitoring me. I'm sure I haven't been fucking up the orders. What's their problem?

❍

I'm late for a coffee meeting with a donor, and the end-of-summer crowd on the street seems like it's personally out to get in my way with their slow walking and gawking at storefronts. I hate being late, and there wasn't even a reason for it. I was at my desk, reviewing the quarterly financial forecasts, but it was like my mind was in a fog. Like I was halfway elsewhere. And then it's two o'clock already and I'm late.

I get to the café and apologize to Ms. Tapia, slipping into that mix of cool professionalism and passionate activism that makes me good at my job, and we spend an hour talking about post-cyclone relief in island communities. She leaves with a satisfied look on her face and I know we still have her support. I pack up my bag, and make for the toilets when I catch my reflection in the mirror behind the bar and I'm struck still by déjà vu. Someone runs into me from behind, and I stammer an apology.

In the toilet, tears spill from my eyes. This sense of longing, of loss comes over me. I've been to this café hundreds of times, looked at myself in that mirror who knows how many times before. Where is this coming from?

I try to get myself together, feelings I don't understand coursing through my mind. And over all that, a meta-feeling of anger at myself for having these nonsense emotions in the first place.

I flush, wash my hands and splash cool water on my face, run my hands through my short hair. The grey patches at my temples are growing, but it looks good. I've never thought of myself as vain, but I know I'm a handsome woman. I've caught myself checking out my reflection, thinking "oh, she's hot," in that fraction of a second before I realize I'm looking at myself. Now, as I look at this face in the mirror, the one I've worn for over four decades, it's like I'm staring at a stranger.

I blink and force myself to go back out to the world, force these stupid feelings down. I pull my phone from my pocket, scroll through my calendar, focus on my work. I glance up, not wanting to run into anyone else today, and notice someone staring at me. They look away when I catch their eyes, but I remember that during my meeting, I'd looked up to see this same person watching us. Watching me.

They have distinctive salt-and-pepper hair in loose curls framing a thin face, and I'm convinced I've seen them somewhere before. They are carefully avoiding looking at me now, staring down at their phone, when it's like the mirror all over again. In an instant I feel like I know this person.

I walk toward their table, no idea what I am going to say when I get there, when they glance up. Our eyes meet and a look of panic forms on their face as they see recognition on mine. They stand and make for the door, and I follow, cursing the maze of tables in this small café. I get out to the street, but they are gone.

۞

Do I even want to know what's wrong with me? It's not as if I don't have enough drama in my real life to obsess over—opening night is only two weeks away, and Marko is on tour in Europe so between work schedules and timezones there's barely any time each day when we're both awake. Not to mention that Ellis is being decidedly weird. Aside from the bare minimum required to serve beers and burgers, they hardly ever talk to me anymore except to interrogate me about whether I'm "okay."

No, I'm not fucking okay, but that's none of their business. Ellis and I aren't friends, we just work together.

I dream about them almost every night. Not Ellis—that couple. Me-not-me and her wife and their domestic harmony. Jobs where they have to wear suits. A house with an actual backyard. Adult children. I can't ever remember the details of these dreams, yet I somehow know this entire backstory. It's like I'm on stage, and I've learned the entire script even though we're only performing a single scene.

Like I've gone full method and I'm losing my grip on who I am.

The worst part is, I like it. I haven't felt this *much* in years. Isn't that why I became an actor, to live in someone else's body for a few hours? So what if I imagined it rather than some playwright. Does it really matter that I'm a little bit in love with a life that isn't mine?

☎

At work preparing a PowerPoint for an upcoming symposium, at home watching Netflix: there he is, in the back of my mind. I can't stop thinking about him, the way he makes me feel in my dreams. And connected to that desire, there's this sense of drama. My career is on a precipice, my personal life is complicated and exciting. It's like I'm on the edge of either becoming incandescent or ruining my life. But it's not me. My marriage and my career aren't what I'd call boring, but they are both solid. The life that's in jeopardy is not my life. It's like I'm caught up in some novel, overidentifying with the main character, her life and my life entangled in my mind.

And it's been going on for months.

But now it seems I have two obsessions—a life that doesn't really exist and a person who definitely does. That person from the café who I'm convinced was trying to get away from me. I don't know why, but I feel like they know something, like if only I could talk to them it would all make sense. I know it's irrational, all of it. I know it's probably just my hormones changing; my sister told me she thought she was truly losing her mind when she was my age.

But Christ, I never thought it would be like this.

Every day as I walk to work, to the supermarket, to meet Thérèse, I scan the people on the sidewalk. Looking for black and white curls. Thérèse caught me staring at a group of people at the farmer's market on the weekend, and assuming I was checking out the woman in the leather singlet, laughed and asked if she needed to start worrying.

"You're not having a mid-life crisis, are you?" she said, slipping her arm around my waist. "If I catch you looking at red convertibles online, I'm sending you to therapy."

I forced a chuckle. "If I start looking at cars, you should have me committed."

Out of the corner of my eye I caught a glimpse of a tall, thin person with salt-and-pepper hair by the stand with the feijoas and it took all my willpower not to run over there.

Please, let this only be a mid-life crisis.

ༀ

Tuesday night, mercifully quiet. The last remaining table clears out just before eleven and Ellis suggests we close early. Tomorrow is my day off and the idea of a good night's sleep fills me with joy, even though I know I will wake confused and wanting. How do you miss someone who isn't even real?

"Sure," I say, loading the dishwasher.

"You want a beer?" they ask, holding up a frosty pint glass. I'd been looking forward to getting home early but now a beer sounds exactly like what I need.

"Why not?"

I set the dishwasher going, and hop up on to a stool across the bar from the taps. Ellis pulls a pint for us each and slides one to me.

"How old are you?" they ask, without preamble.

"What?"

"I'm 46," they say, as if that explains it.

"You don't look it," I say, deflecting, and because it's true.

They grin and lift their beer. "Clean living."

I laugh. I haven't told anyone my real age in over a decade, but it doesn't seem to matter now.

"I'm 43. I guess we're both a bit old for this line of work."

"That's not why I asked," they say, a serious look on their face. "I was about your age when it happened to me. The dreams. The other world, your other life. I know what's happening to you, Immy. You aren't going crazy. It's real."

I should be shocked. I should be terrified. I should quit on the spot and never come back. I don't move.

"Does it get better?" I ask, after a long silence.

They shrug. "Depends on what you think better is. It gets… clearer. If you let it."

"If I let it," I repeat. "So, I can make it stop?"

"If you want to, you can." They finish their pint and hand wash the glass. "I'll be at table seven tomorrow if you want to know more."

○

I finish my report to the Board of Directors on our desalination project and take a late lunch. I go back to the café where I've been every other day for a week in the hopes of seeing that person again. There's no reason to believe that today will be any different, except that I do. And I'm right.

They look right at me when I walk in the door, sharp eyes in a sharp face. A flash memory comes to me: a dark bar, the taste of hops and malt, the words: It's real.

I stare at this stranger who is not a stranger. They wait for me, patiently, apparently unconcerned whether I join them or not. Ellis, I think, not knowing where the name comes from.

I look around at the other people in the busy café. I wonder if any of them can move between realities. I think about the dreams, the feelings pouring through the tiny connection I have to my other self. I can't even imagine what it would be like to throw open that window fully. It seems exhausting. But also exhilarating.

○

It's hard enough to live one single good life. To be present and open, to care, to try to make something meaningful in this world. I know that there's nothing better on the other side, that it's not an escape. I can't escape from myself, from all the selves I could have become. No one can.

And that will be true no matter what I choose. Whether I open myself to my other life or not.

I look at Ellis, sitting at that table, with the key to open or close the window forever, and I know what I want.

BLINK

Darkly Lem

I DON'T KNOW HOW LONG THIS HAS BEEN HAP-pening—days, or weeks, or years. I have memories of a before, and I have memories that I no longer have. Lives I've lived that are gone, barely thoughts anymore, glimpses.

I am in bed, a baby monitor resting on the night-stand next to me. Tree branches rub against the glass, squeaking; I need to cut them back. They've woken me up three nights running. I've been here just moments.

I check the monitor but my daughter sleeps, scarcely moving, breathing balloon breaths. The memory of her birth returns, is with me, always has been. The rainbow bunny we bought her brother to give to her at the hos-pital. The way she holds her feet while giggling after baths, the knowing her, the being with her.

The leaving will be awful.

I know what's coming—I try to keep my eyes open, hold back the fear, the loss, the knowing, the inevi-tability.

I've blinked twice already.

The springs in the bed creak as I roll over to embrace my husband. He smells like charcoal. Like the dog. Like me. He'll shower in the morning, wash it all off and I'll be gone.

It's been so long since I've felt this safe.

It takes two blinks to clear my eyes, to see my husband's hair once more. Only one remains. My husband stirs and rolls toward me. He reaches over my shoulder for the monitor. I smell him more strongly, the sweat of his sleeping, the scent of yesterday, the sunscreen he had to slather on to convince our son to wear it. We stood in the woodchips of the playground the day before and watched our son run up the slide, this time without slipping once.

I want so badly to keep my eyes open, to see my husband's dark shape forever. He starts to yawn, or perhaps speak, and I catch the beginnings of a sound, but I can keep my eyes open no longer.

Ꙩ

I am standing outside a sleep warehouse. So many of us pressed against the gate, the sweet stink of someone's whiskey breath crossing my nose, the heat of all those bodies surprising in the cold.

Beyond the gate, through the chicken wire glass, I can see the bunks stacked atop each other, hundreds of them in rows lining the walls, their sleepers motionless. They sleep for the rich—no, they sleep for the giggers who can barely afford the service. Clarity comes swiftly; this version of me is rested. New knowledge of this place seeps up like water through a flooding floor, overtaking old memories. The sleepers for the rich are elsewhere, places I cannot afford to go, neighborhoods I would be accosted simply for walking down the street. Here, though, amid the refuse and the refugees and the black market warehouses, here I can afford to be. Here, where the sun reaches the sidewalks only now, in the morning. In half an hour it will be behind the platform, in another hour it will be gone, past the horizon of skyscrapers and pavilions and penthouses I'll never see the inside of. Not even if I were here for years.

I remember eating, with my children, my husband. I remember how we grilled yesterday, but I have not eaten for days now because I have no children and have no husband. My stomach twists around itself.

I remember sleeping and not dreaming. I miss that absence of thought, that quiet oblivion. I wish someone in that warehouse would sleep for me. I wish I could afford to have someone sleep for me. But I am here to offer my own body.

The tip came yesterday, just before sunset. We've done this before, the anxious, powerless waiting. There is no solidarity in this fulsome mass, no camaraderie. Three hundred would-be sleepers for three remaining bunks—camaraderie is a luxury of those who still have hope to lose.

The gate opens and a woman slips through the tight opening. Three small lines descend from her left eye, tattoos of the Orillo family, though she is not much better dressed than we are. We all back up instinctively.

"You know the drill," she says. "Three bunks left, if you've taken Edirex in the last week you're out, don't bullshit me, we will be testing on the inside." Her voice is bored but weary, and she looks little happier to be here than we are.

Some people in the crowd grumble, step back.

The sun is beginning to reach the rim of the platform, bleaching the ground near the edge of the crowd but retreating, leaving shadow in its wake. She stands before us, her eyes running over the whole sorry lot of us. Someone in the front acts first, screaming to be picked, and others follow suit, the once-still crowd now snapping to action. The corner of her mouth twitches upward.

This is a real chance for nine hours of oblivion—I'm older, yes, not the most healthy, but still. I step forward. "Orillo," I say, "I'm your guy, Orillo!" My voice blends with the rest, but the name catches her attention. For a second, she looks surprised. She's probably not a true Orillo, but it doesn't matter. The name worked.

"Old dog, huh?" she says.

"Old dogs sleep hard."

She looks me over, then takes my face in her hands, pulls each eyelid down, inspects the whites. I start to smile.

"Stop," she says. She pushes my head to the side, peers in an ear.

"Sorry."

"Blink for me."

"I don't take Edirex. Shit, I don't even pop a Buphy if I'm hungover."

"Just do it."

I blink. Number five, but when I open my eyes she's still standing before me, her fingers still on my cheeks. I let out a shuddering breath. Two more left.

"Okay," she says. "Old Dog here is one. Any other hard sleepers out here?"

I approach the entrance, my eyes stinging. The guard looks at me, grunts, and opens the door. I force myself not to run through and lay on the first empty bunk I see. If I can just get one and close my eyes, maybe I can get some sleep. Wake up in the same body for a change. I am so excited at the idea that I stumble, wasting a blink to right myself.

Fake Orillo is beside me, grabbing my arm, inspecting me again. "You okay there?"

"I'm fine, let's go."

"Hold on," she says, narrowing her eyes. "You've still got to blow on Phyllis before we wire you up." She stops us in front of a machine on the wall, a mouthpiece protruding from it, kissed by every sleeper in here. Beside Phyllis, a row of bunks are stacked toward the chicken wire windows, their occupants sleeping, the peace of oblivion on their faces appealing. The smell of hundreds of sleepers' sweat hangs in the air, mingling with coolant and desperation and the bright chemical tang of the weapons laced to our supervisors' hips. The woman puts a hand on my shoulder, pushes me toward Phyllis, not unkindly but not gently, either. I lean into the mouthpiece and blow. I taste the decay from someone's rotting tooth, the old rubber and moldiness of it in my mouth. Old fingerprints streak down the surface from hundreds of sleepers who came before me. I add my own as I press my palm into the side of the machine to catch myself from falling.

I am unprepared when the green indicator flashes and my eyes fill with light and then darkness and I slip out of the world.

☎

When I open my eyes, I am running in a forest of icy naked tree limbs. Snow is falling around me, my breath sharp in my lungs. I'm cold everywhere and my legs ache. The arrival into this world, into this life, is sluggish. I don't know where I am or who I am. I have been running for a long time.

Blink.

I don't hear anything at first, no hint of where I am, no sign of what I'm running from. But another few breaths and I can hear it: the soft crunch of twigs in the snow. I glance around and the glow of eyes are on me, moving with me. Their pursuit seems effortless and I can hear laughter in the distance. Not human. Animal laughter.

Blink.

I should pick up my pace. But my boots are heavy and my coat is heavy, and I'm very tired. My lungs are burning, scalded by exhaustion and the cold and fear. The shotgun in my hand is heavy too, and I wonder how that was the last thing I noticed. I open it up to look in the chamber—I know how to—and I see that it is empty.

Blink.

I reach into my pockets and pull out two of the shells I know are there and slide them in, one and then the other. My fingers are numb and tingling. I snap the barrel back into place.

Blink.

The eyes are moving ahead of me now, curving toward the path in front of me. They meet there, eight sets of eyes in total and now they're approaching me. Seven are wolves, I can see now. But one is more than a wolf. Man-shaped, with a long muzzle and an open mouth full of teeth. Taller than I am, it is a furred darkness, a solid mass of menace. It stalks behind the rest, but with a leap, it is up above them and over them. Still airborne, it defies gravity, somehow suspended as I lift the shotgun.

Blink.

○

I open my eyes in the dark, blink, and text scrolls over my vision—the time, the date, the weather report. I look left and the text disappears. Right, and there's a flicker, then an image appears, a perfect picture of the near nothingness I see before me.

Then a single spot of light appears far in front and below me and a roar erupts all around. It's people, thousands of them, a whole stadium of people applauding, cheering, as a lone figure emerges into the light.

She stands, perfectly still, as the tumult around me subsides and the orchestra begins. Her hand carves an arc around her, and the crowd draws a breath as one. None of us blink as she begins the dance, modern and ancient, solo in the middle of the stage.

I finally break free of the dancer's spell and notice holographic images of her at the edges of my vision, billboards pronouncing the worldwide broadcast of the performance. But I and several thousand other lucky ones are here to see it live. Here in the largest stadium I've ever seen, filled to the rafters with rapt attention, all on the dancer.

She is graceful and strong, one with the music. I could watch her forever from this hard plastic seat, but my eyes begin to water and I can no longer help myself. My eyes flutter and I blink my last.

○

I am in a crowd. We are protesting. I am protesting. Around me, my compatriots are surprised to see me, and then they are not. Their chants do not stop. Our chants.

We are standing across from an office park, clustered on the edge of a parking lot. People emerge from a building. They are trying not to look at us.

Our chant changes. "No longer human!" we shout together. "No longer human!"

They get in a car, drive away, immortal but discomfited. We are allowed no closer, I understand.

In protesting, there is such clamor and so little movement. This office park is in the woods, not far from a highway, and the smell of pine needles and car exhaust is strong. I am holding a sign. My hands are cold. I have been standing here for hours and standing here for seconds. I wiggle my toes; they are growing numb.

It is no longer autumn, not yet winter. The sky is gray and the trees are bare and everywhere are reminders that life ends, must end. My eyes are dry, my lips chapped. In the middle of this crowd, there is only tumult, but beyond it, past the parking lot, past the cars, past the buildings and the impossible science within them, among the trees and the cold, crunching dirt, there is stillness. I know there is. Between the earth, spangled with sodden leaves, and the impassive clouds, there is stillness.

What a blessing stillness will be.

ↁ

A sky bright with sunlight greets me when my eyes open again. In a blink I'm no longer standing, but sitting, cool breezes replaced by relentless heat. The stillness, at least, persists, and for that I'm grateful.

Nausea crashes through me. Bandages surround this body, hugging every inch of my skin. Other bandaged bodies sit along the same dingy, sand-blasted wall I lean against. Dark purple blisters peeking through where their cloth wraps cannot cover. The same spots cover me, I realize as the dull ache of each one registers. Must be hundreds of them. I moan.

Crowds, crowds, I remember a crowd just a moment before, and further back still, though not like the one around me now.

Everyone in this crowd is wrapped in cloth from feet to face, everyone save the men dressed in uniforms, carrying guns, standing by massive shining metal doors. And one other. A woman in robes, wearing a cloth mask but no bandages. Was that a tattoo, her eye? Three small lines. I blink to clear dust from my eyes but the tattoo is gone. "Orillo," I call out to the woman, but my voice comes out in a wheeze, and then I realize the blisters pepper my throat, too.

I push myself up and take two steps before the aches turn to sharp, stabbing pain. My eyelids squeeze shut as I moan, louder this time, gurgling. I fall back into sand, its heat somehow soothing. I know when I open them I'll be gone, so I keep them shut a few moments more, letting my body's aching wounds rest in the sand's warmth a while longer.

☯

Three of my husbands will return with the sheep this afternoon. I can already hear the dogs in the hills, ready to be home, their brothers and sisters with us pawing at the ground, howling their excitement. The apples are ready for picking, but we await the first frost, the trees still greedily holding sugar, the fruit not yet as sweet as it will be. Oldest Wife says it will be soon; she can feel it in her knees. She sits by the fire, drinking tea and making pasta and says it will be here within the week. Thin, wrinkled fingers work fast, the knife in one hand moving fluidly, without cease. Her knees are rarely wrong. There are many of us—my husbands, my wives, my partners. They are all mine, as I am theirs, as our children are all ours. Two I've borne myself, and perhaps a certain favoritism for them lingers, but they both are good at reminding me of the silliness of such attachments; they are even better Küninists than I, which is why I love them so. What more could a parent want than for their children to surpass them? As my dozens surely will. My heart is overfull, yet with every passing day it swells and love I thought would slosh beyond my borders is held safe, precious and preserved. Who could have imagined such crude beings as we could contain within ourselves this magnitude of joy? I envy the me that will remain, will get to grow old among her loved ones, will get to see such beautiful children become beautiful adults. I envy the me that will get to die swaddled in such happiness. I envy the me that will die. How many families must I abandon? How many is too many? How many is enough? I will not get to see my husbands' return. I will not get to taste the pasta I am rolling, or the apples, hanging heavy just beyond the window. What will it take to say, No more, I wonder. What will it take to say, Stop.

I blink.

♋

I open my eyes to a darkness hewn by the white of my helmet lamp. Detritus from sealife above hangs inert in the black. I am suspended, just now touched by another light that is blue and growing. I strain to keep my eyes open. I feel that I should be here. A lifetime of work has prepared me for this descent into a newly-spawned trench, and yet there is a kind of feedback to my memory. A distortion in my mind telling me that this is fleeting, transitory as ever.

I inhale heliox from my tank, aware of the shuttering nanites from my deep suit's effort to contain what pressures surround me. I know I am down here for a reason, that I belong, but an immediate terror at what might lurk in these depths seizes me. This cannot be real, must not, and then—yes, something comes, emitting that growing blue light, which swells in its approach. I close my eyes. I open them again to find a great creature before me, an otherworldly thing that no version of me would recognize.

"As expected," I hear in my mind. The creature is massive, perhaps the result of abyssal gigantism, but its shape and proportions defy logic. Bioluminescent markings along its toady skin makes a kind of sense down here, but nothing else does. I believe this is a dream or some failing of my brain, yet the voice rebounds in my skull again: "Be still, we haven't the time."

Time? I think, and the voice answers.

"Yes. You have been gone in five or seven, and will be gone, again and again, for however long it requires, five and seven, again and again."

How does this creature know—

"I knew because I will be permitted to know. Call it God, or some simulacrum, but it has had its way. You will learn what you can in what glimpses you have been given, traveler. It won't all be bad, certainly, and there must have been a reason, however unreasonable. You have found it. You will catch it."

The me of this moment feels compelled to ask questions but the bars of pressure, the flashes of memory from someone else, make it difficult to breathe. The heliox seems thinner, which is just as well. Something has to give. This careening is too much. I am forced to flit between worlds and lives and my memories of them transform into deja vu or worse, black spots with their own friction, agitating my awareness in any given moment to near panic—at least I think. I think.

I push the button in my palm to activate thrusters, a habit I barely recognize from training. I propel toward the trench wall, wheeling around and colliding against it. The impact disconnects the tube on the back of my helmet. I don't know what blink I'm on and I don't care. I feel a yawn coming and a buoyancy in my head as the last of my air escapes. I hold my breath and close my eyes.

☯

I can smell syrup. Air is in my lungs, my breath steady. Sunlight angles in from the window above the sink, motes of dust lilting and flaring.

Breakfast foods. Butter sizzling in the pan, bubbles splitting and merging, rich, delicious smoke in my nose. Upstairs, the girls play. Happy sounds of stomping feet and gentle laughter.

The chorus of a song they've been repeating for days.

Lena is in the living room, doing the Saturday puzzle.

"Legendary science fiction writer," she calls out. "Six letters, starts with 'leg.'"

I blink.

"Never mind," she says. "I got it."

"Who?" I ask.

"Ursula Le Guin."

I nod, sliding the pan of sausage around on the burner. I notice a stain on the wallpaper beside the refrigerator. I don't remember what it's from. My heart is beating very loudly. I blink again.

Chives sit on the cutting board, chopped so fine they're almost a paste. My knife is sharp. I am proud of it, fine German steel. Lena makes fun of me, says the edge is more a threat to my fingertips than a help in making food. Says it makes me feel like a samurai. It's not *Japanese*, Lena, I tell her. She laughs and I laugh and I love her so much I can't catch my breath.

And I know there's almost no time left. I know, with the savage force of certainty, what it is I'm going to do. The knife is in my hand, its weight familiar, memories of the meals I've made, the time I've spent with them, shivering within my mind. I am so tired of leaving and I am so tired of missing those I leave behind, and I can already feel it, the absence, before I'm even gone. I miss them already.

The knife is in my hand and then it's on the floor, clattering, and someone is screaming, me, I know, and then Lena, and I'm in darkness, agonizing, welcome darkness, but she is holding my hand and I am holding hers and I won't let go.

❍

The next week passes swiftly. I can't explain to Lena why I did what I did, and if I tried they'd put me away. The psychologists and specialists and doctors all ask the same questions, the one Lena doesn't ask, though it's in her voice every time she speaks to me. I say whatever I can think of to make them let me go. And then they do.

It isn't so bad not being able to see. I can hear all the quiet noises of the house. The slight wheezing of the refrigerator comforts me now, and my children's laughter, and Lena's voice calling me from the other room. I can smell pancakes in the morning and baked ziti at night. I've memorized all the nooks and edges of my home, my little world. My leave from work has been extended from weeks to months. I am receiving disability, though a part of me, this version of me, anyway, worries that someone will accuse me of fraud—but I am free for now. Lena has been doing a lot more around the house and working extra hours at the shop. I feel guilty.

Months pass this way. The kids like that I am home. We play games where I stumble around the house looking for them.

One of the twins is hiding in her closet, I can hear her snickering. Three paces from the top of the stairs, turn left, six paces, turn right, two paces. The laughter grows louder as I get closer. I feel the left wall with my fingertips, taking shuffling steps to avoid tripping on any toys or clothes or books that may be strewn across the floor. Once I feel her bunk bed's frame I turn and cross the floor, hand out, feeling for the doorknob of her closet. I yank it open. "Got you!"

"How did you find me?" Rose asks.

"I used my sonar powers."

Giggles come from farther down the hall and I open my mouth, faking surprise. I can imagine Rose smiling.

"Gotta find Violet!" Rose says.

I let the new giggles guide me, Rose holding my left hand as we move down the hall, singing *we're going to get you, you can't hide.*

I'm in Violet's room now and I already know that she too is in her closet. I yank open the closet door and the laughter abruptly stops. Rose too goes silent behind me but for the hiss of her excited breathing. I squat down and run my hands across the coarse carpeting and feel nothing but a shoe and a forgotten Lego. No Violet.

"Violet?" I say.

"Where is she?" Rose asks.

I call out again. Nothing. I feel around more. "Violet?"

I take a deep breath and stand back up, sending my hands out into the array of dresses and sweaters hanging to my left. There is the catch and scratch of sequins along my palms and the softness of cotton. And I feel Rose's hand on my back just before a new round of giggles erupts from somewhere deeper in the closet. "I was in the trunk," Violet calls out.

"Oh, thank, God! Violet! I thought you had moved out!"

She snorts. "Come on!"

"Flown the coop!"

"Stoooop!" She tugs on the O, stretches it to a whine.

I hear the squeak of the hinge as she steps free of the trunk. I drop to my knees to hug both of my daughters. I hope they remember these moments the way I will.

Weeks later we're in the den. I'm on the couch, Lena at the computer.

"Listen to this," Lena says. I hear the click of the mouse.

"I'm listening."

"There are people who think the world has been changing around them."

"So help me if this is about Jewish bears again…"

"Don't tell me you don't remember that spelling!"

"You're ridiculous. I love you, but you're ridiculous."

"Anyway, it's not about bears."

"You're one stiff breeze away from ranting about the Bilderberg group…"

"It's not about bears! Listen. People think the world is changing around them and they're giving these really specific, weird examples. Some guy is saying Montana used to have a million residents and that Hawaii hasn't always been its own country. I mean, I guess when it was just a colony, right? But they've been independent for…Hey, are you listening?"

"Definitely."

"When did Hawaii declare independence?"

"Just before Guam. That's all I remember from school. Why are we talking about Guam?"

"You weren't listening."

"I wasn't *not* listening."

"And then there's this: 'The house I grew up in now belongs to a very polite old couple. They said they've been living there for 37 years. I'm only 21, returning for summer break. They invited me in and showed me pictures of their time in the house.' Don't you think that'd freak you out?"

"I think I'm a little freaked out by how much you love conspiracy theories."

"This isn't exactly a conspiracy theory, though. I mean, it's just strange. Why would someone make it up?"

"Allow me to introduce you to the internet."

"Like, I feel sure that we had wallpaper last week, right? Remember?"

"Do we not?"

"Not any more!"

"Kind of a crummy joke, Lena…"

"You know I wouldn't make a joke about—"

"About wallpaper?"

"About your eyes."

"I know. I was making a joke, too. Do we really not have wallpaper?"

"It's painted blue. A nice blue, the kind of blue I'd like, but I don't think I chose it."

"Well let's go check some houses in Hawaii, see how their walls look."

"You were listening!"

"To you, darling, always." I sigh contentedly.

There's a silence and I can feel her eyes on me. "You happy?" she asks.

"I am." And I am. "Truly."

Ↄ

A year passes. *More* than a year.

Rose is upstairs playing in her room and Violet is in my arms, head on my chest, listening to my breaths and announcing each one by number. She counts up to seven and starts again. Rose doesn't do this, only Violet. The part of me that has always lived here knows this is a quirky habit of hers.

"Five," she says, and my body tenses. She notices and looks up at me. "You okay, Donkey Poop-head?"

I laugh. "That's a good one."

She kisses me on the chin and rests back against my chest. "Six."

I rub her head absently.

"Seven."

Lena is lying on the couch across from us. I can hear her light breathing.

"What are you doing?" I ask Lena.

"One."

"I'm reading," Lena says. "You need something, Donkey Poop-head?"

I laugh again. "No, just checking on you."

"Stop talking, I'm losing count," Violet says.

"Okay, okay."

"Two."

"This book is a slog. I'm going to the kitchen. You want anything?"

"Thr—"

My hands are resting on the arms of the recliner. Beneath my feet, the rug is dry and soft, and the world lists to one side, though I remain seated. Lena yells something from the kitchen, but I can't understand her. On the couch, Rose laughs. The smell of reheated risotto reaches me, another dinner Lena made. Made for the three of us.

Lena walks back into the room. "I asked if you wanted anything."

"Violet," I say.

"What's that?"

There is a noise in the room, a low, strained crooning, an animal sound, and it is me. I am making it. I stop, but cannot stop myself from speaking again: "Violet."

Lena moves closer to me, the floorboards creaking with each step. "Are you okay?"

I have one child, have always had one child, and yet I feel Violet's weight like a phantom limb, her pajamas' soft cloth, pocked with fuzzballs.

The memories of a thousand worlds tumble through my head, a slurry of terror and lust and expectation. I remember salt and sand and the nightmare of being hunted or left adrift, the quiet times even, the calm of normal life before being ripped away once more, and now again.

I am counting my breaths, hopelessly, desperately, each leaping along with my heartbeat. I arrive at seven. No Violet. The little girl I love, I know, who never existed.

I hold the air in my traitor lungs, let it out. Wait. I can hear the churning of blood in my ears, feel its throb in my veins. Wait to inhale. My body is an engine of flesh and fear. Wait. Wait to see what else it is I will do to this world. Wait. What vertiginous anticipation is waiting.

ON THE SPECTRUM

JUSTIN C. KEY

—Begin Log, K-1217, 2014 Years After The Fifth Flood—

STATIC BUBBLED SOMEWHERE BEHIND MY EYES as I carved out the hole in the wooden number six. Teacher, trying to get me to Telepath again. I scratched my ear and hummed. The static went away. I finished my clock and looked it over. I'd failed every other test assessing which of us atypical Koinos could handle cognition-enhancing medication. This time, I'd make them notice.

A second wave of static came. This one held a faint scent of coconut. Whereas Typicals identify other Typicals by codes, IDs, the texture of such telepathy, I knew April by the shape of her face, the pitch of her voice, and the smell of the conditioner that kept her tight curls from knotting up. I turned to see her walking over from her own finished clock.

"You could at least try to buzz me back," she said.

"I prefer talking," I said, unable to bring myself to tell her that I had been trying. "The vibrations help me think. Besides, we won't need it on Koinos Island."

"You trying to get us Nefratoled?" A fresh push of coconut as she playfully slapped my arm. Koinos Island was a place April had dreamed up where neurodisadvantaged people like us lived independent of Typicals. The now-shared fantasy included a plan to elope there and live in speech-based harmony.

"Teacher's not listening. You'll listen when you go Typical, right?"

"Me? Typical? Not a chance. You seen Rocky's clock? He's next up for sure."

"They almost picked you on the Download exam. What if this is it?"

"I'm more of an islander myself."

April touched the slabs of wood still leaning on the foot of my workbench. Though April and I had been friends since forever, I still learned more every time I looked at her. The way her eyes widened when she was amused, the whites of her eyes expanding against her russet brown skin.

"Extra parts," I said. "But it works. Check it out."

April did. The final test had us recreating, from memory, a three-dimensional mechanical clock. We got five minutes to inspect the model. Its "second hand" mimicked a spaceship's voyage starting at Osiris, curving past one of the moons, and slingshotting back around Mars. Most higher functioning Koinos could at least pull up slivers of living memories, exactly as they happened. For me, memories were more like ghosts. So, I improvised.

My clock's solar system was U-shaped, as if giant hands had folded space onto itself. April turned the cogwheel mounted on the back. Hidden cogs carried the crudely-carved space shuttle from the twelve on our planet, past the four on the Moon, and toward the eleven on Mars. April's eyebrows peaked as the shuttle fell towards the red planet. A faint, distracting murmur rumbled between my ears. She was speaking in that way her mother taught her, the way my own brain was incapable of. I imagined her perception of telepathy was similar to mine, only with some of the static cleared away. Her teeth clamped over her lip, emphasizing her small gap. I had no clue what she was thinking.

Then, when it looked like the spaceship would crash, a hole opened up in Mars and the shuttle fell through. With the solar system's curve, Mars was one level above Osiris. When the shuttle popped out on the other side, April jumped a little. The spaceship started back from home, exactly a minute into its trip. She smiled.

At that moment, all of my deficiencies seemed worth it.

"A hole in space. Where'd you get that idea?"

"Nowhere. Why?"

"It's interesting, is all. You think a real ship could jump around like that?" She looked me in the eyes as we spoke, which meant she was further my way along the spectrum. "You have to show Teacher. It's genius."

"AmLit worthy?"

Amliterone was the new medication that promised to push high-functioning Koinos to Typical. April had let it slip that Society needed more minds to prepare for 'something dangerous from space.' She refused to say more, but the fear in her eyes spoke volumes. It had spread across her temples, down to her pursed lips, and into my daily imagination. Mind-eating creatures; boiling meteorites; an exploding sun. Ponderings about the end of the world kept me up at night.

"You wouldn't be the same on that stuff."

"That's the point. I'd be better."

"Remember what happened to June?"

"The medication is safe by now. It has to be. Besides, if I could Telepath we could talk all the time."

"I like not knowing what you're thinking. This clock was an awesome surprise. I'd be bummed if I just automatically knew about it, for sure."

"I bet space would cheer you up."

April gave a half smile I couldn't quite understand and fingered one of the levers on my clock. I knew she wanted to see the other side of the sky even more than me. But she had already been part of Society, back before she was diagnosed as Koinos. From her tellings, Society was a beautiful labyrinth of ideas, collaboration, instant feedback, and shared experiences. But April often found herself lost in their web, unable to grasp their rebuttals to her fanciful and often abstract views of the world. Eventually, she was cut off.

"Naw," she said, finally. "When's the last time you seen a Typical look up at the sky?"

Before I could respond, a metallic clang made both of us jump. Clang, clang, clang, coming from my clock. It took a second to remember. I had used scrap pieces of metal to build an internal sound-based mechanism to signify specific times. Now that alarm was going off nonstop. To me, such a sound was a gift in an otherwise quiet world. To Typicals, however …

Teacher came. A gritty static wedged its way behind my eyes, blocked out the sound of the chime, and made me wince. I scratched my ears; mental chatter made me itch.

"She wants you to stop it," April said.

I tried to shut the clock off, but the switches weren't working. Whatever I did only made the clanging worse.

"Tell her it tells time just—just like all the other clocks," I said. "Tell her the spring must have come—it's just a little thing, really." I moved my hands as I spoke, something I did when I was excited or the words came out faster than the thoughts behind them. I searched for paper and pens to draw out what I meant, like Therapist had taught me, but of course there were none. Teacher put a hand on each side of my clock. "Tell her to give me a second!"

Teacher gave me two. I watched, helpless, as her milk-white fingers swirled around my clock in a calculated blur. In seconds my creation was reduced to its parts. Her fingers paused a heartbeat, as if considering to torture me with a second chance, and then proceeded to build. She soon handed me the finished replica.

I looked up at Teacher, my hands shaking. I hated the way her face said nothing, blank as the spare slabs of wood. I hated the static coming from April, undoubtedly explaining the intent of the poor, Koinoistic fool, and the return static from Teacher, undoubtedly explaining that there's correct and incorrect and no in-between. I hated how my imagination had allowed even a second's thought that Teacher might have been impressed by my clock's originality.

Most of all, I hated my ability to hate. That, too, slowed me down.

☿

Mother worked in Exploration and took frequent short visits out into space. Father worked on our family's plot of The Farm at the bottom of the hill. He spent his days surveying miles of greenhouses until every ripe fruit or vegetable had been picked and shipped for processing. I learned later he had been raised Explorer. Usually neurotypical children independently tended a family's portion of The Farm as soon as they could walk. He'd been grounded for my insufficiencies.

I tried helping once. Biting an apple was the first time I'd experienced taste—real taste—and it had been like someone trying to speak to me through my tongue. Father's co-farmers found me sitting in the middle of one of the fields, destroying produce with my teeth. I simply couldn't help myself. Father banned me from the farm. I was confined to his modest garden, where the only harm would be our own.

There came a period of time when Father took me on daily trips to have tall people watch me play a variety of games. I didn't know they were tests at the time. Some made me laugh; others were boring. I remembered one vividly, however. The one that taught me what I was.

I sat in front of a screen attached to a writing pad with a color-changing pen. A picture of a satellite orbiting Osiris appeared and flashed away after five seconds. My job was to replicate what I'd seen as perfectly as possible. Photographic memory was usually well developed by the age of three. I was five.

I could remember only fleeting details of the photo; my mind quickly flew in different directions. I drew a sailboat with wings, dancing to the moon. My imaginary friends loved it. Up popped another prompt. I thought Father wanted to see more of my creations.

And then, Mother's static. The crackles were too uniform to ever make anything of them, but they smelled like her skin; I could always tell when she called. Father's static intercepted. Thick waves of radiation roiled around me.

For the first time in my life, something got through. The culmination of Father's frustration, the heat of his anger, and the slow expanse of exhaustion coming from his cortex lightly touched the shores of mine until its meaning was cold upon my skin. He'd yelled at Mother, but I alone felt the sting of his words: "I don't understand him."

He took me home and to my room. He didn't try very hard with me after that.

I don't understand him…

I desperately wanted him to.

☯

The sun had set just enough that its rays shattered into a blanket of rainbows as they filtered through the clutter of sky-traffic. A distant rocket carried a space shuttle silently out of our atmosphere. The satellites and way-stations orbiting Osiris were so numerous that the daytime sky sometimes rivaled the night's for constellations. My own dreams of flying had been short-lived. My brain couldn't work fast enough to travel at their speeds, and the world had no intentions of slowing down.

April stood quietly with her arms wrapped around herself. Her eyes were red from tears. My heart swelled. Another failure for both of us. We were stuck together.

I wanted to say something, but we shared a campus with Typical children. We were already labeled by where we stood, waiting, as if a minute or an hour or a day of our short lives was insignificant enough to waste. Talking brought unwanted attention. So I took out a piece of paper and began to draw.

A long, slender orb of light detached itself from the lines of flight overhead and descended from the sky. The flying vehicle stopped soundlessly a few feet in front of us and the door slid open. April's mother looked over and waved. It had taken many of these brief interactions to realize the grimace on her face was an attempt at a smile. I liked April's mother. We understood little of each other, but she had a way of making me forget that.

As April passed, I pressed my note into the palm of her hand. I caught a sliver of her eye. Then she was gone.

I sighed. The world moved too fast.

Another thickening line of light came down to materialize into a vehicle that was somehow familiar even though it was exactly the same as all the others. Mother looked straight ahead as I fastened myself in. Her skin was as white as Teacher's and just as hairless. She wore the same thing as all Exploration Typicals: gray overalls with white shoes. Her static crackled against my distracted mind. The ground speeding away and the tall buildings shrinking to toy-sized blocks fascinated me every time.

The buzzing intensified. With some effort I opened my mind a little to Mother's probes, something I worked on extensively in Speech Therapy. She knew of my failure through Society. What she didn't know is if I'd tried.

Of course I had tried. Of course I wanted to talk to Mother in the way Brother could, to feel her ubiquitous, loving embrace that had soothed him as a baby even when she was in orbit. Of course I wanted to know April's thoughts instead of agonizing over the millions of possibilities behind her eyes. Of course I wanted Father's understanding. AmLit, these tests, all of it—just hopes, wishes. And I failed.

Before I processed any of this into a proper response, we were home. Time was another great separator. For me, only the length of a fleeting thought had passed. For Mother, the time wasted had been much longer.

I followed Mother into our dwelling and halted at the sight of her now naked skin, softly reflecting the grayed sun-rays filtered by our home's screen protectors. I looked away. Though my family never wore clothes in the home except for sun-alert days, nudity continued to make me uneasy. Perhaps it was the vivid memory of Mother and Father creating Brother in our communal area while casually connected to Society, shown by the glassy look in their eyes and the slight tilt of their heads towards the heavens. I thought Mother was attacking Father with her hips. My distress didn't cause them to stop, but rather to disconnect from Society and try to soothe me while continuing their act. April's amused explanation only worsened my modesty.

I retreated to my room and reassembled my clock, without an alarm. It didn't take long. I put it with my collection: buildings that transformed into bridges, two-headed beasts with parking lots in their stomachs, structures I saw outside my glass walls, in my school, and even floating in front of the moon on a clear night.

At seven o'clock, Father brought my daily Nefratol. Instead of three pills, there were four. I almost tried to ask why, but I knew. I handed Father my clock. He looked it over so quickly I didn't even see his eyes move. He placed it on top of one of my constructions and left. No confusion. No disappointment. No, "I don't understand him." Just indifference.

I spat the Nefratol out. By blunting my taste, blurring my vision, and slowing my thoughts, the medication eased the stress of a home not built for me. Instead of waving my arms when words weren't sufficient for meaning, I simply didn't speak. Instead of drawing on my bedroom walls to combat the confusing uniformity of everything, I sat and watched sky-traffic. When I was on Nefratol Mother would talk and I would listen. I often wonder if, for her, those were our best times together. For me, it was like missing a part of life.

I didn't want to talk to Mother that night. I wanted to talk to April.

☯

Before I met April I didn't know I had a voice. Two Typicals held me down in an empty room during Break while a third taped long wires to my hands that were connected to small boxes emitting an alien hum. Static swung heavily between my captors. With no way of communicating, I could only squeal against their grips.

I felt April's static before I saw her. My fear rose; more Typicals meant more experiments. When she walked in I immediately placed her keen eyes from some of my classes. She always wore colorful clothes that stood out against grays and blacks.

She casually removed the wires from my skin while the Typicals looked on. I stared at her, open-mouthed, as broken static flitted by me. She grabbed the small identification screen Mother clipped to my belt each morning and held it up to her head, then showed one of the Typicals.

The boys looked at me, then April, and left.

"Your name's August." She held up my ID and pointed to my date of birth. "See. Awe-Gust." Though I didn't understand the words at the time, I never forgot them; they were the first I'd ever heard.

April taught me how to speak. When she was first diagnosed as Koinos, her Historian parents hired a speech therapist specializing in vocal sounds. I often hummed to fight off the quiet, or to drown out residual static. April showed me hums could be words and words could have meaning.

A room with shelved walls filled with fragile artifacts called 'books' crafted by Koinos-like minds, long before telepathy or Society existed, became our new playground. I marveled at April's history lessons. The art, the creativity, the very fabric of their Koinos civilizations, so different from Society. What's more, I understood them. I understood how different parts of the world could choose disparate ways of life. I understood how people could choose partners based on feelings rather than genetic compatibility. Sitting there, drinking April's words, for the first time I felt what Mother and Father and Brother must have felt linked to Society.

I even understood the vices that brought Koinos their own destruction. Conflict, wars, poverty, famine, the permanent damage to Osiris's atmosphere that turned our only sun into a brutal tyrant. Writings on this great change and the resulting Flood were scant, and mentions of Typicals (referenced to as 'special', 'extraordinary', or 'savants') even more so. One brief text on the history of modern civilization commented that only spread out patches of people survived after the Flood; genetic drift selected for the once 'extraordinary' ability to communicate over vast distances.

When I could speak in a full sentence, I finally asked April the long-burning question awaiting my voice: what had she said to the Typicals?

"I told them you didn't want to be part of their experiment."

"That's it?"

"That's it. They didn't realize you had wants. Once they did, the only logical thing was to stop." She laughed at my look. "Typicals aren't so bad once you understand them, or they understand you. Their whole life is just one big equation. If you change one variable, you can change the way they think."

I asked April to explain what the word 'variable' meant. She did, and I smiled. Maybe it wasn't so bad being atypical. April made me proud of the way we saw the world. I thought we'd see it that way together forever.

♋

East Lake sat lost in the shadow of the City. It was too shallow to act as a source of water, the land around it too soft for farming. To any logical Typical, it was useless. That's why it was perfect.

April was waiting for me on the shore, soft waves cresting her half-buried feet. "I got lost," she said. "I thought you drew a swimming pool."

"I'm a builder, not an artist."

"Next time try building some directions. Or even just, 'the lake in the east.'" She kicked a clump of mud into the receding water. "I talked to Teacher."

"Oh?"

"She felt bad about the clock. She thought she was helping."

"Big help."

"Were you able to put it back together?"

"I was."

"Good. There'll be more tests when they make a stronger med. There's always new meds."

"Good news for one of us, at least."

April smiled a sad smile. Before I could fully place it, she moved her hand toward the water, prompting my gaze to follow. "Is this where you come to think?"

I picked up a flat rock and skipped it over the water's surface, trying not to look at how the setting sun fell on her brown skin. "This is where I come to stop thinking."

Once the last sliver of sun succumbed to the horizon, April laid her clothes in the sand and stepped into the water. She waved me in. I hesitated. Refusing would remind her how different we were. I stripped to my underwear, hoping that was normal enough, and followed her into the lake.

Wrapped in my thoughts, I lost my footing and flailed to keep my head above water, splashing April in the process. She shrieked and, before I could apologize, a retaliatory splash broke against my face. We spent the next ten minutes—an hour, maybe an eternity—chasing each other with walls of water, clumsy and falling over ourselves, delighting in each other. April ran onto shore. I pretended to untangle my leg from lily-pad vines to give her time to dress. I dared a look; she was still exposed, only drier.

As I made my way back, I noticed the neat, tight curls of her hair. Her coconut conditioner caused it to glisten in the dusk. Right before my hips broke the surface, I felt myself swell. April waited; if I stopped she'd know. I focused past her and on the City. I brought up images of Teacher dismantling my clock. Though blurrier than anything a Typical would produce, emotion filled the cracks. That helped.

She pushed me, playfully, before I could reach my clothes. I made after her; she jumped away. We ran, continuing our game from the water. We pretended I was a merman and she an evil sailor trying to sell me for cash, then that we were the last two people on Osiris, destined to save the world.

"Koinos Island," April said, her breath heavy and harsh from running on the wet sand. She spread out on the ground. I lay beside her, pushed my shoulder softly into hers. "Just you and me."

"It would be paradise. No more itching. No more quiet."

"Can we go?"

I made to get up. "Let's go right now."

"I'm serious, August. I didn't make it up. Koinos Island, it's real."

"Can't be. They're all dead, remember?"

"Some Koinos survived the flood. They're still around. I thought finding it was the fantasy. But maybe it's not. A place where everyone talks like us, creates like us." She took my hand. "Can you imagine?"

I couldn't. Koinos, living independently? How could anyone ever get anything done when they could spend the day lying in the sand, wondering what the person beside them was thinking?

"The world is passing us by. And with…" April bit her lip, glanced up to the sky.

"Tell me. I can handle it."

"Society is trying to get everyone off Osiris. All of us. They say what's coming will destroy the planet."

"Aliens?"

"Worse," she said. "Way worse. A hole, in the sky. In the stars."

The air had been thick with static lately, a world buzzing with excitement out of my reach. Was that it? Was Society scrambling to save itself while oblivious Koinos like me tried to reinvent the clock?

"What's any of this have to do with Koinos Island?" I said.

"I bet they're trying to figure it out, too. What if they can beat it?"

"No way. Whatever is coming, Typicals will figure it out."

"Society dissected every idea I offered before I knew I even had it. I was like a rogue ant, wandering off the path, going against the colony." She shook her head. "Your clock was brilliant. What if we could escape through that hole?"

"Illogical."

"To Typicals, yes. But on Koinos Island? We could be a part of something. I need to be a part of something, August. I can't live in the in-between like this. What are you doing?"

I stopped snapping my fingers next to my ear. "Sometimes the quiet gets to me."

I picked up our clothes to busy my hands. Something fell and rolled in the sand. I froze when I saw the blue plastic casing and the pills shifting inside.

"You passed?" I said. I picked up the bottle of AmLit, the miracle cure for Koinoistic Spectrum Disorder. The pills were so small. So lifeless. Yet each of them had more power than I could ever possess: they could give April what she truly wanted.

By the time I held it up for my only friend to see, we were both crying.

"Congrats," I said.

"I was waiting for the right time to tell you. I don't want it."

"What do you mean you don't want it? This is it. You can be happy."

"You make me happy, August."

Then, just like that, her lips were on mine. She tasted of tears and something more, something indescribable. I pressed back, my body more sure than I was. I didn't know what it was like to connect to Society, but I imagine it felt a little like that. Images flew through my head. I felt a million things at once.

"Run away with me, August," she said again. I searched her eyes as she searched mine. She was serious. If I said yes, we'd go, right then, and never look back. "Please."

"I'd love to." I handed her the AmLit bottle and stepped back. "But there's nowhere to go."

☯

Run away with me.

There's nowhere to go.

I spent that night lying in bed, wishing I could take my

words back. April's revelation had come while I was lost in a sea of my own emotions, trying to grab on to the flotsam of fragmented thoughts about islands and speech and the sky opening up. When I saw the pills, my heart was stunned with the horror of being truly alone.

Thinking through emotion is like running blindfolded. When she asked me to leave the safety of Society, fear led me the wrong way. That blindfold now lifted, I saw the truth: anywhere would be better than here. Better than AmLit. And we'd be together.

April's square was empty the next morning in Math class. Was I too late?

Society knew. I was literally floating in their telepathic waves. I concentrated on tapping into those answers until my head hurt. It was like trying to see more stars in the night sky just by straining your naked eyes. You know they're there, you know their light can reach you, but no matter how hard you try you can't see them because your equipment just isn't what it should be.

ପ

I saw her after school, but she wasn't waiting for her parents. She crossed the grass in long strides, carrying a portable computer designed for telepathy. Maybe I had her confused. This girl wore all white instead of April's usual colors. But I knew that skin anywhere. The memory of her face was the closest my brain came to photographic.

"April!"

But she moved fast toward the gated parking lot designed to keep out wandering Koinos. Desperation pulled at muscles both physical and mental. I pushed all I had to get something out telepathically, to finally reach someone when I needed to most.

April climbed into one of the flying cars; her eyes swept over me like Father's had over my clock.

And then she was gone, into the sky.

ପ

A year passed.

New medications ushered in new tests. I was never chosen, never understood. My Koinos classmates melted away. Soon the tests went away, too. One day there was no school. Only home, with Father and his farming.

Mother left for months; I had no clue why. The air grew frenetic with static. Sometimes I woke in a night-sweat, fully expecting Typicals had left me and any remaining Koinos behind to fend for ourselves.

In a way, they already had.

Ω

A pause, then static. Therapist always tried telepathy first. Sometimes I appreciated it; other times I felt like some broken thing that he kept trying to turn on.

When I didn't respond, Therapist took out his electronic canvas and handed me a pen and paper. He'd shown me that drawing was common to people across the spectrum. Sometimes, when Therapist drew something that couldn't have been from a memory, I wondered if he was a little Koinos himself.

He drew a picture of April in Explorer white, mentally jotting down notes on her tablet inside the Mars space station. I cringed; she was all wrong. I took the picture and was meticulous with my edits. April had a glow about her, especially standing in the sun. Her eyes were not simple orbs that absorbed light. They were windows into her. The her no one else had gotten the chance to see.

Run away with me.

I showed Therapist the result. He looked at it briefly, set it aside, and then drew what looked like a satellite image of our solar system only with a dark, vast hole in the middle. Space seemed to bend toward the void. Therapist circled it, as if I was too dense to notice. This unknown menace was responsible for the fear that had driven Society to take April away. And for that, I hated it.

I responded with a picture of me and other Koinos children sitting in silence, ignorant and helpless. Then I wiped the canvas clean. What was the point?

Therapist drew a picture of me in Engineer blue. I puzzled over it, thinking maybe he was punishing me for my emotions, until he brought out a blue bottle. He opened it, took out two of the shiny blue AmLit pills, and placed them on the table. No, not AmLit. The coating was smoother, the sides angled. This was new.

My pencil flew across the page. Therapist let me have the moment. Then, not unkindly, he took the paper away. I had drawn a feverish depiction of a road, littered with my failures, leading away from Society. Therapist responded with another picture of me in Engineer Blue and gestured with the pills.

I considered a moment, then wiped my canvas and went to work. Sparing details for speed, a few minutes later I held up a crude drawing of a boy and a girl playing tag along a lake's shore. "If I 'get cured,' will I be able to come up with this?" I said.

The silence that followed was so long that I thought the session was over. As I stood to leave, Therapist began to draw. The same image of me in Engineer blue, this time walking past a room with Koinoistic children playing. I recognized them by the wideness in their eyes and the joy on their faces. In the picture, I didn't seem to notice them.

His message was clear. If I got cured, I wouldn't want to.

♋

What was I waiting for? April to come back? I rarely saw her. When I did, even in her rush to do Typical things I thought her eyes paused on mine. For just a second, like when a ball rolling downhill hits a crack in the cement. I wanted those eyes to save me from having to decide between losing myself and being alone.

I thought about those eyes as I sat in my room, popping the cap to the medication, pushing it back on, popping it again.

Why choose me now? Was this some last ditch effort to expand Society by any means? Would this new medication destroy enough of me to ensure I wouldn't be that ant leading the colony astray?

My dream of being selected had become a living nightmare.

Ͼ

I'm taking the pill. April couldn't live like this and neither can I.

Will I be happy when I change? How could I be, passing April every day and not caring?

Indifference isn't happiness. But it's better than this.

—End Log, K-1217, 2014 Years After The Fifth Flood—

Ͼ

Engineer-1217 shut off the log. He took a minute or two to mentally replay the telepathically translated text a few hundred times. Despite being able to pull exact memories from his brain like a hard-drive, he'd always found that nothing quite matched the initial sensory experience. For that reason, he listened again.

E-1217 had done well. As Head Engineer, he had advanced spaceflight tremendously. A thousand generation ships were set to leave the solar system and seek out a new home. There were potentials in various stellar systems, the closest only several thousand light-years away.

When, twenty years ago, Society had detected the strong possibility of a wandering black hole appearing in our galaxy, the goal was to migrate Osiris's entire population. But with no habitable planets in the Milky Way and not enough time to terraform anything close, this was the logical end of the equation. All in all, one percent of the population would be saved. It was the best survival all their calculations showed.

So why did he feel like it wasn't enough?

The doubt started when the small but resilient Koinos colony living at 35°N, 139°E reached out to collaborate in building what they called a 'stargate.' Society knew about the lost colony well, along with their absurd ideas and fallacious understanding of basic physics. Unless the independent Koinos were willing to undergo treatments, any meaningful interaction was seen as a waste. Society needed strength in unity, not wandering ants.

This dismissal disturbed E-1217. As a Typical, he had become completely logical. He wouldn't be dissatisfied with Society's plan unless something was missing. E-1217 waited until just after sunrise when the largest portion of Society was either asleep or tired of mind to run the numbers. Despite the current consensus, the increase in mind-pool alone couldn't explain the benefits of adding Koinos. Even after medication, there was something inherent about them that improved the group's cognitive abilities.

E-1217 pulled out the clock that had been stored with the log. It was an interesting design. He had failed a standard Replica task and instead had created a shortcut in the solar system to make up for a lack of speed.

This could save us, April had said.

Fantasies can't save anyone. Society knew that. E-1217 knew that.

Why then, years later, was he so fascinated?

He replayed April's words, well aware he sought more than meaning in the ghost of her voice. She an Explorer and he an Engineer, their paths never crossed after E-1217 joined Society. And without the legal ability to pass on their Koinos genome, there was no logical reason to pair. But they were always together. They explored the trenches of each other's thoughts, replayed interactions from their past lives with deeper insight into themselves through another's eye, and delighted in shared experiences. Remnants of their disability stayed alive through love; neither ever felt alone.

From his workstation, E-1217 was still with April during a routine fly-by of Mars. The duality of Koinos awe and Typical analysis from seeing the red planet through her eyes was poignant. It lingered long after the rogue asteroid collided with April's ship and blinked her consciousness out of existence.

He replayed the moment a million times over. The error in the asteroid map, the kinetics of the inelastic collision, the dismantling of her biology all made perfect sense. Then why couldn't he understand?

E-1217 spent days in this state of repetition. The medicine's effect melted away; cresting emotion eventually broke over him. By the time someone found him, he was a dehydrated shell of himself, begging for meds to take the pain of her away.

He hadn't missed a dose since.

But…

E-1217 listened to the log again. He looked at the data and opened the part of his mind linked to Osiris, felt its past, glimpsed its future. The wandering black hole was set to appear in the solar system some time within the next two to eight years. He looked at the clock. He went over their current plan. He tapped into Society, felt their peace with it, looked into himself, and wondered…

He was missing something. Society was missing something, even as they were missing nothing. But he couldn't find it. His brain just wasn't equipped to envision it.

Logic told him that only illogical thinking could get him there.

He stepped out into the garden, which had died shortly after his Father. He unscrewed the cap of the pills that had given him new life over the last twenty years, and threw the bottle into the night.

BATTLESUIT

Cliff Winnig

THE BATTLESUIT HANGS READY FOR ME—A CO-
coon, a carnivorous plant, a Georgia O'Keefe
flower. I stand naked before it and wonder
how it'll feel to merge with the thing. Once you're in,
you're in. That's it, soldier. Welcome to the cyborg elites.

The suit smells of machine oil, metal, and lilac. I
didn't expect that last bit, but I know it's partly biotech.
Maybe it looks flower-like for a reason.

Here at the end, they leave you alone with it, I guess
so no one can say you didn't choose on your own. Still,
you hear stories. Some soldiers close their eyes and leap
inside, afraid they'll lose their nerve. Others just stare
at it, sometimes an hour or more, before the MPs come
and take them away. I heard one guy even went fetal.

Not me. I'll do my duty. I'll step into the suit, let it slide
its needles into my spine and the nerves that run down my
arms and legs, let it enfold me for the rest of my life. It will
protect and hold me. Parent, lover, weapon.

I step forward, surprised I'm breaking into a cold
sweat. Well, that won't affect the connection.

I take another step.

"Jon, no!" A voice echoes down the hall from around the corner. Katie, my kid sister.

I should enter the battlesuit now. She'll get here just a little too late. No messiness. Problem solved.

Instead, like a putz, I wait for her arrival. It doesn't take long. I have just enough brains to wrap a towel around my waist before she bursts into the room.

Hands on her knees, Katie gives me her spiel between breaths. "Jon. Don't be stupid. I know you miss Liz. Really, I do. Losing her sucks. Okay, I get that. But that's no reason to graft yourself to this…this…Wow, it looks even creepier hanging open like that."

She stares at the battlesuit, aloof in its alcove. The rows of spines shine in the harsh fluorescent light.

"You don't even like needles!" she says.

I frown. "They say you don't feel them, like acupuncture." She shouldn't be here. We said goodbye yesterday, during my last meal. "Civilians aren't allowed in this part of the base, and women definitely aren't allowed in the men's locker room." She'd run through it to reach the suit chamber. "How'd you get in here, anyway?"

"I called Uncle Steve."

That makes sense. He's been a DC lawyer for decades. He's got connections.

"Guess he doesn't want me going full cyborg."

"Let's just say I got base access in record time. He didn't even kvetch about the pro bono work."

"That is out of character. Must have really not liked the idea."

"Can you blame him? He said he'd be losing his favorite nephew."

I shake my head. "I'll still get leave."

"That'll be great. I can see it now: home for Passover, and you stand around like a suit of armor, unable to eat, unable to sit without breaking a chair."

"So what? You always hated family meals."

Katie rolls her eyes, like she did as a child. "That's not the point."

"Tell Uncle Steve he wasted his time." I watch her face sink. "I've made up my mind, Katie."

She changes tactics, giving me puppy dog eyes, like she's about to cry. She's still got freckles. Makes her look younger and adds to the effect.

"You're not ten anymore. That doesn't work." I hope she believes me, because it's starting to work.

"What will, Jon? So Liz walked out on you! It was hardly shocking, what with all that depressing stuff you painted after Somalia."

"She used to love my work," I mumble. I look down at my feet, then back at her face, at the battle there between hope and loss. I reach out and brush a stray hair from her cheek. She's warm and a little sweaty from her run through the base.

Katie meets my gaze. "What I mean is you pushed her away. You don't have to keep doing that. Just find someone, Jon. Find someone and don't push them away."

"Katie, I know you don't want me to do this, but I've thought about it a lot. Liz was right. I'm not really husband-and-father material, not since the war."

The images come then. Dead soldiers, dead villagers, families. They say once you're in the suit, you only see what you want. I can't wait.

Katie takes my hand, squeezes it. "Don't talk like that. I know you're in pain. I've lost people too."

I pull free. A second later it hits me she's just talking exes. "It's different," I say. "When you're married."

She looks away, but not at the suit. "Maybe it is."

"It's not just Liz, okay? It's the war." I glance at the battle-suit, silent witness to our conversation. I wonder if its helmet cams are already recording. Years from now, will I watch myself arguing?

"Katie, you're so worried about how different I'll be once I'm in the suit. Don't be. I'm already different."

She looks again like she's about to cry. "I know. Of course I know. But really, this is kind of extreme." Now she does look at the suit, her face hard, like she's sizing up a rival.

"I've already tried therapy, Katie. There's nothing else left."

"What about your art?" She's like the enemy, constantly changing tactics.

"I haven't painted since Liz left."

"I hear it's therapeutic."

"So's ripping apart tanks."

Footsteps echo down the hall, coming fast. A couple of lightly cyborged MPs jog around the corner and head straight for us.

"Step away from the battlesuit!" shouts the closer one, a redhead. "Now!"

We both step back.

"Not you, Sergeant." Red frowns, shaking his head as he comes to a halt beside me.

The other guy grabs Katie and pulls her away from the suit. Naturally, she struggles. He gets her in a half nelson, and she quiets down.

"Hey!" I shout. I move toward them but halt when the MPs turn as one, staring at me with chrome eyes.

"Jon! Get this guy off me!" Katie twists around to glare at her captor. "I have permission to be here."

"You have permission to be on base," he says. "But you're still not allowed in the suit chamber, or the men's locker room."

"Told you," I say.

Katie gives me a look. "I have the right to talk to my own brother."

"Sure," the MP says. "When he's done suiting up."

This gets Katie's hackles up like not even the half nelson did. "Suiting up! He'll be locked up for life in that iron maiden!"

I know what she means, but I think of the band. Growing up, I spent hours with Dad's metal collection.

At a nod from Red, the other MP drags Katie away. She's kicking and screaming, but it's useless. Red follows them out. I watch them go, but I'm thinking about the battlesuit. I've just remembered it streams music right into your brain, along with the endorphins. I see myself, powerful and effective, as I crush enemy skulls to my own personal soundtrack. The new soldier—unafraid and never alone.

A wave of longing flows through me. I turn from Katie's diminishing cries and let the towel drop to the floor. Before me hangs the battlesuit.

Chrome. Solid. Beckoning.

With just a hint of lilac.

I walk toward it, arms wide.

LIFE AT SEA

CRAIG LINCOLN

WE NEVER THOUGHT WE WOULD LIVE LONG enough to make it to our transmission day. I watched you go first. You lay on the black padded table with countless nodes stuck to your skin, all those wires and you, naked, save for one of those unflattering gowns and the weighted anklets. You made it to your 75 ½ year first. We laughed at the half-year, seemed so arbitrary. "Meet me in Aruba," you said. We had done so once, before, when we first met at a destination wedding there. You were there for the bride and I for the groom. And after that wedding we were there for each other, for forty-six years.

Aruba was underwater already, the rising seas reclaiming it as the world keeps warming. Humanity thriving as the world was dying. We used to find ourselves sitting in the dark, staring at the wall, talking about where we should go to find water in the same manner we used to talk about where we should go for brunch. We yearned for something to believe in.

Life at Sea offered hope. You and I figured, why not

try it. Do a little more than just eat vegetables and wish the world would come together in our twilight hour.

We applied for Life at Sea like others might buy a lottery ticket, just on the off-chance. To put our hats in the ring. We knew we were ideal candidates—over seventy years of age, no children, no siblings—but the concept was so outlandish. For months we heard nothing and even forgot we applied until our packets came in. To our surprise, we were both accepted and had to submit blood and urine, which made it feel real. Even so, we half expected to die in riots or from starvation before we made it to minimum euthanasia age, you in three years and me in four.

The monitor blinked to life, status bars filling once your transfer initiated. Cables ran from the monitors back down through the floor and into the water below, where a vat of algae awaited.

"Whoa," you said. "Trippy."

I was about to ask when the monitor confirmed the transfer was complete. A needle on an armature shot into your thigh and you sighed—breathing out, but not back in again. You went limp and a door in the floor opened, your body fell in and sunk into the water.

One of the techs came over and handed me a clipboard.

"That it?" I asked.

"That's it," the tech said.

I signed and walked away, expecting to cry but unable to. Instead I just felt hot and raw, knowing a copy of you was out there, somewhere, living inside an algae bloom.

❈

Scientists said willpower was the key, some unquantifiable drive to press on and survive. That's why housing human consciousnesses inside the algae somehow increased its reproduction by 350%. I tried not to think about it, not with having to wait for another year to join you. I wish I could tell you that year was easy, that somehow the temperatures started dropping, that all the tech they came up with finally saved us and we started cooling. But I never could lie to you. Even when you asked if I wanted kids. I tried to lie then but had to be honest and admit I did, though the thought of bringing a child up during the fires and famines was more heartbreaking than denying myself the chance at watching one grow.

I'm not proud of how I made it through that year.

A year in our lives before the fall would usually pass in quick, broken moments, without many events worth remembering. Not this one. My brain, fogged with age, remembered the abandoned shack we would drive by, that I would tease you with, call it your retirement home. The joke returned to me in fully realized cruelty when I spent my year on its dirty floors, wondering if I ate enough yesterday to go without today, once sleeping on top of my knapsack to hide it as drifters shined their light over me, hoping they wouldn't see me, or if they did, that I looked dead enough to allay any interest, and, other times, getting heart flutters and praying to a God I didn't believe in to let me stay, let me live just a while longer. But more than that, the year reminded me of the lack, you, felt in each silence that hung over me, silence only broken with my talking, to nobody, just to make sure I remembered how.

My worst shame came when I broke into a house with a family. Husband, wife, two kids. I raided the pantry, sobbing quietly as I loaded up cans, made it out without a trace. I hope they still made it, that my theft was only a setback. No way to know now. Probably for the best. I survived, please forgive me.

Life at Sea was still in business, my contract intact. I didn't believe it until I lay on the transfer table myself. The room looked less…shiny than it was when you went. A sort of grime coated everything. Only the techs were in the room with me when they flipped the switch.

There was a feeling of falling, followed by a cold fluidity which passed over me. I could no longer see. My body experienced a sort of weightlessness, unmoored from the ground. Minute grains enveloped me like a hug. Something dropped from above, and I felt the shape of it as it fell through me. I knew at once it was my body, and even tasted some of it as it fell, weighed down by anklets. A loud, steady hum rumbled through my flesh and a current pulled me outward.

There was a rush and I can't say things got brighter but everything did feel warmer, so it all *seemed* brighter. Pins and needles ran across my strange new flesh as I drank in the light. I imagined it must be the sun, that familiar heat distorted by the water.

Other blooms lingered around, no doubt recently transferred subjects. I tried communicating but had no way to make sound. I wished to scream at them, to find out which way Aruba was, but had no mouth. All I had were cells. Those I manipulated as I could, brushing against other blooms, but gleaning nothing save for the musty, metallic flavor of their flesh.

From behind I felt familiar vibrations, like a voice, echoing down my skin. Words came along them, like someone speaking through cotton. They were instructions on how to vibrate my cells in such a way as to create sounds and send them out.

Thank you, I sent out.

You're welcome, the other bloom said. *Victor?*

I was.

I'm Phie, short for Sophie. Life at Sea asks me to help newly transferred subjects with communication and orientation.

Do you know how to get to Aruba?

I'm afraid I don't. I suggest following the warm currents. Aruba is in a very warm section of the ocean.

My wife is waiting there.

I hope you find her. Seems like you have a plan. Please check in regularly, per your contract, at this location.

Phie was then gone, sucked away down another current perhaps, or off to help another bloom. I kept growing and stretched myself, looking for warmer waters.

You were out there, somewhere.

When night came I longed for the sun to come back, and when it did it fed me with warmth and light. My nights and days came and went, equal periods of longing and ecstasy. Still, I never forgot you or Aruba. I couldn't say how much time had passed or how far I'd gone, but I was aware of being more. My size had increased to the point that I was aware of it in more than one place. Hard to explain. I felt myself being devoured by krill on one end while wallowing in sunlight on the other, simultaneously. I shivered with delight.

ᴔ

More cycles of longing and ecstasy. I find sunken islands below me but none are Aruba. All day I chant your name as I float around, increasing my mass. Zara, Zara. No responses from any other blooms. Hard to tell if any of them were ever human to begin with. I wonder how many more days and nights will pass before I find you. I hate myself for not spending more time memorizing the currents and mapping a path. Has it been years?

I arrive in Aruba. It takes weeks to verify this, swimming above, looking at the shape of the sunken island and comparing it to the shape I spent every day of my last human year studying from all orientations. And yet, you are not here. I wonder why that could be, and my cells tingle as I think of the possibilities.

Were you eaten? Have you found another companion, one like me but better, or worse, or different? Perhaps the transition left some memories out, and our plan didn't survive your transformation. Could you be out there, searching for me, aching to remember where we should meet?

I think of leaving, but Aruba remains forever linked with you. To the connections we made. To leave would be to break them, and to break them, a betrayal. Months pass. Even the warm water licking at my cells offers little comfort, pleasing as it is. Still I remain. Where else is there?

Victor? I hear through the water.

My cells tingle. *Zara?*

A rush comes as another algae bloom combines with my own, the sunlight cascading a pleasure across both of our bodies so intensely that it is hard to tell if I'm feeling it or if the other bloom is. Maybe it's both of us.

I missed you, you say.

I missed you, too, I say.

We stay together like that, our cells mingling, comfortable within each other. When night falls the longing for the light is lessened while you are near. We talk to ourselves, barely needing to vibrate due to the close proximity. We share our journeys: you were almost wholly consumed by a whale, I got lost on a shore until a powerful tide pulled me back in. How strange and wonderful life is, even like this. I spend countless moments like this, within you. Years, probably. I find it hard to find where your body is and mine is not. We are one. Victor and Zara. There is no difference.

☡

We make the child without thinking. We both know it's what we want and finally feel safe enough. We eschew a part of ourselves with minimal consciousness and leave it on its own for a time. Then we bring it in close and name the bloom Sacha, after your grandmother. We continue.

Sacha communicates with us, and grows as we grow. After some time Sacha re-enters us and the process begins anew. We grow larger and larger. We teach other blooms how to do this, and they grow as well. And they teach other blooms. Separating, then rejoining.

More cycles of longing and ecstasy, but no longer measured by the sun. Instead, measured by the forming and reassimilation of our children. Our bliss is timeless.

☡

We thought the making would become boring, one day. But we learned new things each time we split. Our cells stung as they tore from ourselves, and we watched the panicked struggles of the new form, trying to learn to move in this new state. We felt the other algae blooms watching us, the scent of jealousy stinging our olfactory cells like ammonia.

We formed appendages to encircle our creation, to protect it from those who watched, but we couldn't keep the secret. Others learned to split, too, to make children themselves, and they did so at the same furious pace. So we all kept splitting. Cycles of ecstasy and longing but tinged with pride in creating.

♋

Moving has grown somehow more difficult. There is more weight to the water, or more mass to churn through. We are frustrated by the slowness. We cannot go through the sea without touching other algae cells. We worry about losing ourselves and keep ourselves close.

Time and time and time goes by.

The water feels colder and crowded, more solid.

There is a thought somewhere that we might've known this would happen, but can't seem to find it. The memory is lost, if it ever existed in the first place. The waters are thick with us and moving grows more difficult. The cold also slows us and we can feel ourselves withering. There is too much of us, absurd to think soon there'd be more of us than water in the ocean.

We are dying, we think. Slowly.

We figure something will fix this.

We say, just one more child. What could just one more hurt? We split another piece off in our own image to carry on for us because Humanity can't help but thrive. We watch it grow. The sunlight brings less ecstasy than before but there's still a thin layer of it, just enough to taste.

Our child shivers in the light and we feel it ripple through the water and across our flesh. We feel the child with our cells and marvel at its perfection.

THE OTHER ME

REBEKAH BERGMAN

I SAW MYSELF ON THE JUMBOTRON. LOCKED eyes on my eyes looking elsewhere. It was that moment before you recognize that it is you, in fact, staring at you. Before you think, *Look at that. That's Me.* That split second before you begin to wave and do not stop until the Jumbotron moves on. It was a lucky catch, that moment. And then I waved at the Jumbotron. I did not wave back.

So it was the opposite of when you see a stranger walking toward you in a hotel lobby. When you drift left to get out of her way. When you realize that it's not a stranger. It's a mirror. It is Me.

This other Me was taking longer than usual to recognize herself. The thing about the Jumbotron is it's patient. And so am I. I stared at the Me not staring at me. No one else in the stadium seemed to be looking. It was just me. Me and the Jumbotron and this other Me.

My face hovered there, huge. The nose stretched longer than my nose. The lips, they thickened and paled. In short, time passed and the face stopped being mine.

So it was both like and unlike hearing the name of an old lover. How it lingers, enlarged, distorted. And you struggle to tie it down to anybody you know.

REMEMBER, WORDS, REMEMBER

BEN MURPHY

THE STARS ARE DISTANT NOW, AND DIM. THE universe has grown cold and sluggish, and what was once near no longer is. All will end, as motion slows and ceases, even time and God and hell. I sit and wait and think of you.

You once asked me, "When you gaze out over the lip of everything, into the space beyond existence, can you see the back of your own head in the distance?"

"I don't know," I lied. "I couldn't bring myself to look."

The future did not come as we expected it to. There were no flying cars or moon colonies. There was no hyperspace, no holodecks. We cured cancer. We built prostheses. We invented chemicals that stunned and thrilled our brains. We, narcissists as ever, conquered ourselves before we conquered the cosmos.

No one even realized we were in the future. No one knew it would look the same as yesterday, that we weren't going to wake up one morning to find that to-morrow had arrived. It came as so many things do, in the guise of luxury, an indulgence for the enfeebled wealthy, something I rolled my eyes at when I first heard about it then promptly forgot. You and I were living together, that much, at least, I am still certain of, and our lives went on unchanged, love-laden and commonplace, while somewhere some rich old man had started growing younger.

☯

"When your face is upside down you look like an alien. Especially if I only look at your eyes. It's really creepy but also kind of cool. Bodies are so weird."

☯

The population began shrinking when our scientists pronounced us immortal. We weren't, of course, but with enough money they could make us so. People abandoned their children, stole from their parents, betrayed their loved ones, all so they could afford what eternal youth cost. You and I were young, and we went childless, as so many others did, and we worked hard, as so many others did, and we earned enough to live forever, as so many others did not. It was such a small thing, so quick and painless; it took less than an hour. We could even go home that same day. You are not invincible, they made sure to tell us, but you will no longer age; time cannot kill you.

And much as the future felt the same as the past, so was immortality indistinguishable from life before it. We still went to work, and traveled, and fought, and made up, even as our parents grew old and died, and our friends grew old and died, and their children grew old and died, until gradually no one had kids, and no one grew old, and no one died. We ageless few were all that remained, time made toothless by our science, the earth's population a fraction of what it once had been, billions turning out to be not such a big number after all. And life continued, tomorrow endless, eternity quotidian, immortality made mundane by the force of our living it.

✪

"We need to try more foods. I'm pretty sure we have really boring tastes. How sad would that be? If there's some delicious food out there that we've never tried because we think it's strange? I don't want there to be delicious food out there that we've never tried. I want there to be delicious food that we eat. All the time."

✪

What did your hair smell like? Made-up, marketable scents, like hibiscus pomegranate? Like jasmine almond? Like passion fruit essence? As mine did? Or dusty sweaters in the winter, and languorous Sundays.

I don't remember.

The fleshy machinery of my brain proved unsatisfying long ago, and its replacement has begun to fail. What I am is now diminished, and my humanity, for so long suppressed and unnecessary, returns, as I forget how to be anything else save what I was born as. My mind is shutting down, piece by piece, module by module, and memories of you disappear, leaving nothing except a gentle tug inside me and the vague feeling that once I had known more. As you fade, as I fade, I remember what it means to miss you. I wish that I could not.

Blank spaces of months, then years, then whole, weary epochs have been laid to rest in the darkness of my failed recollections. In their place all I have are the letters you wrote me, delicate anachronisms of some synthetic paper, old-fashioned even when you wrote the first of them, a way of saying what speech moved too fast for. Some you wrote while I was light-years away, others during those times when we slept side-by-side.

I hold them now, each page curlicued with handwriting I don't recognize as yours, and read them.

"The sun is warm here," you wrote in one, "and the water is cold. I can't wait to see you, and guilt you into swimming with me, even if it's only for a few minutes. As long as we both get at least a little wet we can still dry out side by side on the beach. And you know that's my favorite part."

Far-off stars wink out with a murmur, though in truth they have been gone for much longer, and I have been more alone than the sky lets on. My own star will burn, for a little longer at least, quiet and hopeless and dim, until it won't.

If I once knew sunbathing was your favorite part of swimming I no longer do. I don't even remember going swimming with you. I can picture it, the way you splashed in all at once, the way you slapped water at me as I waded in slower, the way you laughed when I tried to tackle you, and tugged at me underwater, pulling me in to kiss you, to taste the salt on your sea-slick lips and feel their welcoming cold, the way the tip of your nose pressed into my forehead, the way your freckles hung darkly on your cheeks, the way your toenails were garish with purples and teals as we sat on our towels, the way you cried when we found out later you'd lost one of your earrings in the water, the way you smiled when I gave you one of mine, the way you wore it, your face made lopsided as you tilted your head, how you were so beautiful I had to look away. But to claim that I remember it would be a lie. I don't know if this is memory or fantasy, the scene genuine or conjured by your words. I can see it clearly, but have no confidence in its truth. I don't even know if you had pierced ears.

But how could I be unsure? Did I not hold your earlobe lightly in my teeth, did I not breathe softly on it to make you shiver, did I not trace the line of your jaw with a finger, letting it come to rest gently beneath…what? Did the abrupt coolness of the earring's dangling metal stay my touch, or did I continue on my path, curl up around your ear and into your hair? If I could remember this I could reconstruct all of you, perfect and vivid, unblemished by my erosion. I'd begin with your ears, following them down to your neck and along your shoulders, past your elbows, past your wrists, dwelling on your fingers for long moments, memorizing their feel beneath my own then sliding down your thighs, your knees, your shins, until I have completed you at your feet. But I do not know if you ever painted your toenails, though I feel certain that once I did, so now in my maybe-memory you bury your toes in the sand as we sit by the water.

☯

"I shiver whenever I kill a bug. I'm sharing something with you I've never shared with anyone. Is that strange? Either the shivering, or the not telling, I guess. They both seem strange."

☯

When our species finally took to space in earnest, we found the cosmos was closer than it seemed. The frantic scrabbling that had defined us, the desperate urgency, they were gone. With time no longer finite, we explored the emptiness between the stars, took trips whose length would've been measured in lifetimes, back when the word had meaning. Existence opened up to us and we traveled far, spuming on reality's surf, washing against the universe's edge, an ever-eroding shore.

Eventually humanity reached its limits; we found our minds could retain no more. Our brains weren't built to hold all we wished them to. Time may have been infinite, but we were not, and so we changed ourselves once more.

What we found insufficient was replaced by what was not. We made our minds faster, our memories deeper, our bodies into forms more abstract. We made flesh as obsolete as time, and became greater than what we had been. But when I think of you, it is from before our transformation, though I know that now you have no ears to trace, no toenails to paint, no face for me to forget. Of the little that I remember of you, even less has remained the truth.

☯

"You have amazing eyebrows. Has anyone mentioned that to you before? I don't think many people notice eyebrows specifically, the way you do eyes, or a nose, or lips. But I notice eyebrows and yours are great."

☯

"I'm sorry for what I said," you wrote in another letter. "I didn't mean it, it was untrue, and it was unkind. I just miss you is all. This has been really hard for me. I can't fall asleep without hearing you breathing next to me. Please hurry back."

I could renew myself, carefully, methodically, one system at a time, but I already know it would not help. Energy spreads itself thin across the universe, egalitarian to a fault, and there is too little left for me. I don't know what you said to spark this apology, and I never will.

If I could hurry back to you, I would, but I don't know where we last met, or how we first met. I don't know how long we've been apart, or even how long we were together. All I have left are slivers of the life we led, like splinters, a prick in the skin, the certainty that there is more beneath, and the impossibility of grasping any of it. We fought, as time went on. The reasons why are darkened by the penumbra of my forgetting, but I know we fought. Of all the memories that chance, in its caprice, has deigned to preserve, why did we have to be yelling in so many of them?

☯

"Your jokes can be really mean. You think you're being funny but you're just hurting me. Do you do it on purpose? Do you even notice? I laugh because I don't know how else to respond."

☯

What we are is not what we were, yet we've remained ourselves—we, the few remaining denizens of a universe stretched thin by forever, each of us our own Theseus, and each of us our own ship. I'm sure there are others out there somewhere, though fewer than there once were. Death cannot be cheated, as it turns out. Only delayed. And so when all the stars are spent and every half-life's over, it will find us, ended, along with all the rest. As that moment draws near, some have chosen to preempt it, to cease their functioning and enter into oblivion. Should we say it's suicide, or simply a foregone conclusion, long-deferred? I wonder if you're among them.

We never pondered eternity's terminus, but as it approaches, we are alone, all of us, the knot of lives undone, its braid unwrapped, time and distance and familiarity unweaving it. We remade ourselves to be as limitless as our lifespans, to keep, to be, everything we wished. We were misguided. All things have their limits, and our faultless forms were flawed. I have forgotten even what I am. In the mirror of my mind, I can no longer see myself, only the human I once was. I can't say what it means to hold your letters in my hands, for I know I have no hands to hold, and yet that is what I do. I have regressed, the most basic kernel of who I am, the totality of who I was, now all I can conceive of.

Did being human always ache so much?

Once, when blood ran through me, and I still saw with my own eyes, I could think of little else but you. You filled my thoughts, your touch, your taste, the way you held yourself. The sun that set behind you, that may have slipped away, but your shape against its glow would stay with me forever. I wanted them both, though, sunset and silhouette, so I changed myself to save them.

And for a time, it worked. For a time, I had all I wished, every moment of our lives together, any moment I chose to keep. But for a time is not forever, though once it seemed that way. The sunsets are gone, and you'll soon follow, victim of my greed. Of all else that I've lost, would that I had forgotten what forgetting means.

If I could choose again, I'd keep my body, if only to remember yours.

☯

"Do you even enjoy being around me?"

☯

How was it that we separated? Why? I can't say. It has been lost in the trickling leak that was the past, melting away when the warmth of my memory tried to grab hold of it.

Were we elliptical in our relationship, brought close by the gravity of want only to be flung apart by the momentum of our desires, their force too strident to allow us a more intimate orbit? Tethered by our need, did we begin to spiral back together at our furthest remove, an equilibrium of happiness only possible for some brief interval?

Or was there a discreet end point that we were approaching, each conflict more explosive and trivial than the last? Did we feel the inexorable waning of our attachment, and simply choose to ignore it, to postpone, at least for a little bit, the inevitability of our dissolution?

The final dated letter certainly has no sense of closure about it, nor do any of the undated ones. We simply drift off into the nothingness of the unrecorded, and end as all things will, with a whimper, amorphous and unmoored.

☯

"I don't like being around other people if you're not there too. It doesn't feel right. It feels like I'm only half there, that there's some other half of me that would understand what I'm saying better than whoever I'm saying it to. You're the other half, in case that wasn't clear. Don't let it go to your head."

Ⱋ

Stasis bears down on the universe. I can feel it coming, a quiver, or its lack, the faintest breath of stillness, the eternal exhalation of motion. Reality winds down, and you're not with me to witness its finish. Not even in my mind.

You are something else now, not yourself, a presence, an implication scattered throughout my recollections, coloring them like some heretofore undiscovered hue, a fugitive frequency from a forgotten spectrum—not red, not blue, but you. Were you there when I first watched a star supernova? I can feel you beside me, in the moment before the flash, lingering but faint. A ribbon of you has threaded its way through every realm of my mind, as if, rather than simply disappear, you have dispersed, sacrificing your form, your definition, to find some diffuse ubiquity within me.

You are an emotion. A feeling of creeping shame, of wounded love, of pride and disappointment, of regret and hope and comfort. You are petulance, and desire, you are a dozen kinds of mirth. You are the adulation of justified dread, the preening of I told you so, the warmth of a hard-won familiarity. You are everything that has filled me up and made me tremble with things I have no words fit to describe, for a thousand different reasons, across a thousand different lives. And you are fading.

The letters are before me. This is what they say.

"Why do we do this? I can already hear you asking 'Do what?' three planets away. You know, though. Why do we argue about the stupidest things that neither of us care about?" reads one.

"Did you know that spendthrift means the opposite of what it sounds like? It should be someone who is thrifty with their spending. Not the case! You already knew this, though, didn't you? They should be called spend-not-thrifts, I think," another says.

"You are my best friend. Best friends have fights. You are my lover. Lovers have fights. You are my partner. Partners have fights. But you are still my best friend, and my lover, and my partner."

"You're the worst at taking recommendations. You know that right? The absolute worst. Why do you feel like you have to discover everything yourself? Other people have good taste too, you know. Other people like me."

"It has been the greatest blessing of my life to know you. I thought I should tell you that. No pressure to keep it up, or anything."

"I'll never get used to zero-g. I don't know why you like it so much. It just makes me feel nauseated."

"Would you still love me if you knew I was mean? Because I'm afraid I'm mean. Sometimes I get bitter at other people's successes, or just think mean things at them for the smallest provocation. This worries me. I don't want to be mean. I'm not mean, am I?"

"It makes me sad to think about how long I lived my life without you. And in the same way, it makes me sad to think about a time when I will no longer know you. And I'm sure that day will come. The future will last long enough that we'll find ways to break each other's hearts. So if I seem sad to you, it's only because I know I have never been as happy as I am right now, and I will never be this happy again."

You are gone.

I sit still as the universe ends, an elegiac static. I hold a bundle of letters. They are all addressed to me, but I do not recognize the name of the sender.

Time turned its back on us, so we turned our backs to it. But time did not neglect its duties, and while we waited through what we thought were ageless ages, it silently crept past. Everything will end now, only the rime of millennia will remain, barren of barrenness, empty of emptiness. All is cold and dark, as the last star sighs its entropic death.

And I wonder if right now, in the waning moments of existence, somewhere someone holds, in hands forgotten by me, things that I have written and asks what I am asking. Who wrote such sad, childish, beautiful words?

ARRIVALS AND DEPARTURES

Josh Eure

Now

HE HASN'T BEEN HURT BY HIS CAPTORS AND HE doesn't think he will be. There are two of them, but only one sits with him in the van. He is in the rear seat and she's in the middle.

"The zip-ties aren't necessary," he says.

The woman smiles and the beauty of it pains him. She leans over the seat and cuts him free with her knife.

"Thanks." He twists his wrists around. "I've been expecting you."

"Not me, surely."

He adjusts his legs, which are beginning to cramp. "This whole year actually. I didn't know who you'd be or when you'd come. I wasn't given the particulars."

"That's a funny way of putting it. Given."

"Sure. But if you knew the places I've been. Things I've seen."

The woman nods. "It's why we're here."

"Right. Your little society. That I don't know much about. As I said, not many particulars."

"Well, this isn't exactly official," she says. "I'm looking for answers. To the big questions. But our organization has—well, we're on our own, you might say."

"I see."

"Do you have answers for me?"

He leans back in the seat, enjoying the cool of the AC and the music of the agent's voice. "I have some. Maybe we can help each other."

August 3, 8:22 A.M.

This wasn't his life. His wife's hair was now brown, and she was bonier than the one before. Chris stood in the doorway of their bedroom, looking at this new woman under a white blanket. He knew that they went to graduate school together. He knew that he loved her the first time she admitted she hated a story he wrote, but Chris also knew this was a lie. He awoke to her just that morning, his fortieth birthday. And just like every other birthday, the world around him had changed.

Chris walked into their kitchen to make breakfast. As he whisked the eggs in a ceramic bowl, he stared out into their backyard. The green of the freshly mown grass was bright and yellowing in the August sun, the noise of cicadas managing to make it through the closed window. The fence was stained, and of course Chris stained it, but that too was a lie.

"Chris," his wife said from behind him. "You're making breakfast?"

He turned back, smiled dutifully. "I wanted to let you sleep."

"You didn't have to do that. It's your birthday." She came and gripped him around the waist and rested her head on his back.

"I'm working the late shift tonight," he said.

"Don't remind me. You need to quit that job. Stay home, write. Get a book out there."

Chris exhaled loudly, tired of a fight they'd had many times. "We can't all be as lucky as you, Grace."

She released him and he could hear her footsteps on the tile.

He continued to whisk the eggs.

"You think all of my success is luck?"

"I don't want to fight," he said.

"And I do?"

Chris set the bowl on the counter and moved around her and into the hallway. He grabbed his shoes from the mudroom. "I'm taking a walk," he said, closing the front door behind him. He sat on the steps to put on his shoes, certain that this time would be different. Because this year, he had a plan.

Now

A man knocks on the window of the van and points to his watch. The woman nods to him. She turns back. "We need to be certain that you are what we think you are. We're risking much. I need you to help me out."

"I said we could help each other."

"Tell me about your last life. The one you left before coming here."

He leans forward but she doesn't look worried. She's used to getting what she wants. "I didn't come here. I was forced here."

"By?"

"Who can say?"

"You knew about us. I find your knowledge to be oddly selective."

He sits back again. "You're right. It is. But I'm not the one selecting."

"I wonder," she says, "if you're stringing me along. You're not telling me something."

"And what aren't you telling me?"

"I'm telling you we're short on time. Which you know." She closes her eyes for a moment.

"I can travel, and you want to use that."

"It's nothing so sinister."

He holds up the cut zip-ties. The other captor paces outside in the August heat, his dark skin slick with sweat.

"Well, my partner there is less trusting than I am. He's used to chasing people. They so often run."

"You going to give me something to run from?"

"That depends."

"On whether I am what you think I am. Not just a traveler." The woman smiles.

"You want to know about my last life," he says. "Well, I want to know about your current one. Forgive me if I have trust issues of my own."

August 3, 8:36 A.M.

Chris walked the sidewalk of their neighborhood, passing the duck pond stocked with brim and bass and raccoon perch for children to catch with their Disney-themed fishing poles, and he felt like he remembered having children, so many, but how he lost each one with the passing of another year. He remembered it, but not the way you remember something that happened, rather something more like a dream, a nightmare he recalled in some detail. Chris still remembered nightmares of lives he lived in worlds maddeningly similar to this one—worlds where the streets were named differently, where McCarthy was Tate and vice versa. Worlds where he lived alone in a two bedroom in downtown Raleigh or with a wife and two kids in a five-bedroom outside D.C. There had been a design corralling him, that much was clear. Always a kind of him, America, east coast, around this time. Except—there were also other worlds.

He crossed the highway and made his way behind the Exxon station, passing the Country Kitchen and the nail salon over to the Food-Lion, already teeming with shoppers at 8 A.M. A wash of cold air-conditioning hit his face, icing the sweat on his forehead and neck. The white sodium light and the smell of fresh bread was calming.

Chris walked the aisles. He went through the produce section and then the condiments, thinking of the job he'd had for six years. The job he would go to for the first time just after noon. In this world, Chris was a lineman at RDU. It was absurd, a man with his condition working at an airport, handling arrivals and departures. Someone or something was in control, and they were clearly having fun.

The job was also a big reason that he and his wife often fought. She was a successful writer and now he was a disgruntled one, wearing his blue collar in defiance of what? What was his point?

He completed his trek down the aisles and moved to the registers. He grabbed a bottle of cold brew from the fridge and let the door clap shut, entering the line behind an elderly woman with a puff of white hair. She turned when she sensed someone, and Chris smiled. She smiled. The cashier scanned the woman's items—shampoo, peanuts, bananas, Vaseline, a frozen pizza, tomato paste, milk, cough drops, and Chris was amused by the likely way this woman shopped—from aisle to aisle with no list, remembering and forgetting and remembering what she forgot while forgetting what she needed. The aimlessness was familiar.

"This it?" the cashier said when it was finally Chris's turn.

"This is it. Unless you've got suggestions," he said, winking. Apparently, he was like this here. But, sure, why not? He wasn't long for this world.

"I'd get one with sugar. Those cold brews taste like potting soil."

She was an attractive woman, a redhead, who seemed to be around Chris's age.

"You've tasted potting soil?"

She laughed. "You know what I mean. I prefer it hot, really."

He put on just the right smile. "Is that so?"

She laughed again.

Chris glanced at her name badge. Kelly. "I'll remember that, Kelly. I'll remember Kelly likes it hot. Maybe we can see about getting a hot coffee sometime."

"Sure," she said. "What's your name?"

"Chris."

She wrote her phone number on a card she pulled from beside the register. He knew this was something he would ordinarily never do, but this was the new him too, now—revolution against his fortieth year living in as many lives and as many worlds, with no control over the comings and goings. No say in the destination.

Now

The business of flags makes his head hurt. "If you got a flag or whatever on me, can somehow track me, then why can't you tell?"

"We know you travel, as I said, but we're looking for anomalies. And I suspect you might be one, but my friend out there's not so sure. He thinks you're a black runner from interstitial space with stories and time to kill."

He opens his eyes wider, feeling the AC deep in his sockets. "I have no idea what any of that is. Wow." He checks his watch. "So, I'm an anomaly. What's that mean?"

"We don't know that you're an anomaly. And if you are, it means—among other things—there's little-to-no intel on you. Nothing to track. Other groups seek you out, even if ours chooses not to."

"So now you're on your own trying to get an anomaly before some other society does. And I'm the lucky lab rat."

"You'd be a source of data only. Anomalies travel in any number of unpredictable ways. Some when they laugh or cry, others when they feel shame. And the places they can go are on the margins. One is said to have traveled every fifth and seventh blink, which we assume has something to do with an illogical musical time signature. That's the thing. Little details someone threw in."

"Sounds like I'll be in a maze with cheese."

The woman takes a deep breath. "We need to better understand traveling—its purpose, who makes it happen, and why. The assumption is that anomalies give us the best chance."

"Because?"

"Their peculiarities bely reason or whimsy on the part of their creator. With enough data, we may find patterns. A motive even."

January 8, 9:03 P.M.

An old winter jacket lay in the alleyway, damp and muddied in a pool of rainwater that reflected a slow creeping of clouds above. She waited. She hoped she was disguised well enough by her hood. Were she to be recognized—she set that aside as she noticed the shadow of a man entering at the opposite end of the alley. There was a slight misting of rain, steam billowing in rolls from a vent on the brick wall.

"Hear nothing," she called out, waiting for the expected response.

"It's me," the shadow said, stepping closer. Once the light revealed him, the agent knew she was safe.

"It's 'go see', Jason. There's reasons for the words."

He smiled. "It rhymed."

The two embraced and she was filled with a deep sorrow as she smelled his dark hair, the damp skin of his neck.

"Took me some time to locate the asset," he said.

"How long?"

"Been idle five months now."

"Shit, Jason. This one's on a timer."

Jason shook his head. "I know. It's not an exact science. Couldn't be helped."

"We'll be waiting that long just for approval. Longer even."

"Maybe."

"It's been years since the last one." She turned and scanned the streets beyond the alley as a large SUV rolled by, hissing water up from the asphalt. Its headlights were two blades dartled by the growing downpour. She pulled the hood of her jacket closer. "Where?"

"States. North Carolina, outside Raleigh."

"Anything else?" she asked, turning back around.

"It's not your typical case. It took me this long because of the trail. It's weaker than any I've seen, nearly impossible to track."

"I assume you got a flag in place?"

"Course," Jason said. "Wouldn't be here otherwise. But like I said, this one's different. Been somewhere wild, so now the trail's thinned to almost nothing. I figure it won't be long before it's gone."

"And the asset too," she said, raising her head to the sky. She let the raindrops drum at her face and closed eyes. The cold and shock of it, the sudden lucidity. She lowered her head. "Good thing I have you."

Jason looked to the wall beside them, and she placed a hand on his shoulder. "Thank you. Keep off comms, lay low. I'll be in touch."

She left Jason standing there and walked into the street, hurrying along the sidewalk toward a vehicle idling nearby. She wondered if this was even worth it anymore. Jason believed that it wasn't, that breaking from the company was dangerous and likely fruitless, but he stayed for her. She supposed that he loved her still. But that was another life, another world. The agent knew there were answers, truths out there to be found. And she intended to find them.

Now

He massages the side of his neck, sore from his abduction. "I've only ever lived in what you call an 'unstable world' twice. I remember them both much more clearly. Still like a dream, but they'd been so strange. The first—the atmosphere of the planet catching fire once a day, us underground, eating mushrooms and rodents. My mother kept me comfortable. I never went out or did anything. I ate and slept and watched films through a display on my wall. I pissed and shit in a vacuum that shot my waste to God knows where."

The woman laughs and the sound comes too quickly, startles him. "I'm sorry. No, please, forgive me."

"It's funny?"

"It's just, that's quite an image, isn't it? Where'd it go, do you think?"

He says nothing.

"Fertilizer, probably. Oh, and I bet the mushrooms—right, sorry. Please, tell me about the second one."

"The second one was worse."

"That's it? Just worse?"

He looks out the window beside him to a sky filled with stars and winking lights from aircraft on approach. "Anyway, it was in that second one that I found a fix for my problem. A heading in the storm of my life I plan to follow to its end."

January 11, 5:09 P.M.

Chris was on the tarmac waiting for yet another plane to taxi to their hangar, feeling the cold wind on his hands. He was warm in his coveralls but the Bacardi helped.

February meant an increase in the number of planes requesting deicing, which had forced Chris to work overtime almost every night that month. He ignored the divorce papers on the small card table in the efficiency he rented because he would be gone soon enough. He told himself that whatever version of him was left behind could deal with Grace. Most days though, he missed her.

He spied the small Cessna on its path from the runway, ambling within the yellow lines of the taxiway—a T240 TTX, though he shouldn't know that.

Chris used to wonder about his first life, the one he was born to. He wondered what sort of mother and father he had and if they'd lost a son in his going, or if he'd been replaced by some spiritless copy. Chris was five when he first realized what was happening to him. He awoke on his fifth birthday expecting to see his mother, but instead he found himself in a strange room surrounded by siblings he'd never met. They laughed at his confusion, an older brother slapped his head, told him to quit playing. Chris spent that year trying to figure out what was wrong, what had happened. Whether his former mother was the dream or if this was a nightmare. That ghost of his first remembered mother was the only one he ever mourned. But Chris has clarity now.

He raised his marshaling wands as the aircraft turned. He thrust the wands backward and he stepped back too, signaling the pilot to park in the open lane. Chris chocked the nose gear and another lineman, Tammy, chocked the wheels under the right wing. The engine cried and spooled down, and Chris ran a hand along the slick fiberglass of the left wing, recognizing his buzz. Tammy grabbed the tug and drove it over. She stopped just in front of the plane's nose, and the pilot left them to their work.

Chris hauled the towbar from the lane beside them and Tammy just sat there in the tug, its engine idling. She wore a hood and the dark out there was growing, but he could see her grin.

"What?"

"You're a company man," she said, blonde curls hanging around her shoulder.

Chris placed the pin in the tow-bar ring on the front hitch of the tug, and the bell noise of it satisfied something churchy in him. He wanted a moment of silence.

"Because you love this shit."

"That right?"

"You pet that wing like it was a woman."

He gave her a thumbs up. Chris walked out to the left wing as Tammy reversed the tug slowly, pulling the plane toward the T-hangar. He walked with her, watching for obstructions.

"If you like planes so much, why don't you get your license?"

"I don't like planes," he said, a little too loudly. "Just feeling the rum."

Tammy laughed. She understood.

"Clear on that wing?"

"Clear," he said. "Hold up. Let me move over."

Tammy stopped the tug and waited for Chris to make it to the other wing.

"Okay. You're good."

As they pulled into the warmth of the hangar, their supervisor came out from the breakroom. "Only one wing-walker?" he barked.

"We're fine."

"Hit something and we're all fired."

He headed over to the opposite wing and helped them as they maneuvered the aircraft to settle beside a large Falcon near the back of the hangar, its yawning third engine like a ribbed eye—the biggest aircraft in there that night.

"After you put things away, Chris, punch out and head home. I need you in early."

Chris unhooked the towbar. "What for?" he said.

"VIP for 7 A.M. arrival."

Tammy slammed the hood of the tug. "Who is it?" she asked.

"Don't worry about that," their boss said.

"Is it Bon Jovi?"

"No, it's not Bon Jovi."

Tammy huffed in the cold, formed a thunderhead of breath before her. "Can I come in too?"

"No, you cannot."

"Why? I'll switch shifts with someone."

The man chuckled. "Why do you think I want Chris for VIPs?"

"Because he's a man," Tammy said. "And in my experience, you all look out for your own."

She wasn't wrong. About that place, that world. Their boss often left her out.

"Jesus. No, Tammy. It's because Chris doesn't care. He does the job, doesn't gawp and make a fuss."

"I won't make a fuss."

"No."

"I'll be good. I'll be like a whole other person."

"I said no."

Now

He checks his watch again. Fifteen minutes before the year is up. Before he slips from this world and into another.

"You know of a way to keep me here, but why would I stay? To be studied by some secret society splinter group of two? Kidnappers, no less."

"Fair point," the woman says. "But I assure you, our interests align. There's no telling where you'll end up next. And that world you came from, the one you won't tell me about, it damaged you. You might not survive another trip. And even if you did, we'd never be able to find you. We're your last hope."

"Hope." He lets out a short breath through his nose. "I agree to help you and you'll anchor me here?"

"It's a bit more involved than that. It'll take doing, but yes, we can keep you here."

He thinks about that. Even if this wasn't his original world, it was stable. And there was Tammy.

"And the people you work for? What do they say?"

The woman lays her hand on his. "You don't need to worry about them."

January 12, 7:13 A.M.

Chris left for work earlier than necessary because Tammy had stayed the night. Her two boys were with their dad and she came over with tacos. The time they'd spent and the things that'd been said on liquor made a fugitive of Chris.

It was still dark out as the Gulfstream rounded the corner of the taxiway, lights under the fuselage glaring, and Chris could see the massive turbines and the great T of the elevator, the wings reaching out with their blinking red and green beacons. They parked the plane on the empty ramp and drove conveyors and baggage carts to the rear hold, a fuel truck on the other side where Chris began fueling. The process had become routine, even in the six months he'd been in that life.

Chris toggled between both wings to balance the fuel before reaching the right numbers. He disconnected the nozzle and dragged it back to its cradle, grabbing his clipboard to record the details. He scarcely noticed as the pilot opened the cabin door and lowered it. The man stepped down and stood to one side. Chris looked up. And he watched as a pale woman in a green coat descended the stairs. She wore a dull yellow scarf, her blonde hair flying out in the wind. It was Cate Blanchett.

Chris tossed the clipboard into the cab of the fuel truck, but before he could get in, he heard someone calling out. He turned to see Cate Blanchett walking toward him. Tammy would have loved this.

"Hello," she said.

"Ma'am."

"Sorry, I—thank you for doing, you know, all you just did."

"Yes, ma'am."

"Right. Yes, well. Do you mind if I ask—what did you just do? I mean, I know that was petrol, right?"

"Jet fuel, yes. Something like that." She was in front of him, and he could smell her perfume. Something sweet and French.

"How's it work, um—Chris?" She read the name on his badge, which dangled from a lanyard. It reminded him of Kelly from the grocery store months back. He thought he should call her.

"Just hoses and buttons, really. Third grade math."

"The hose looks heavy. And that big metal piece."

"You get used to it."

"Certainly," she said. "Well, thank you." She held out a folded bill.

"Oh, that's not necessary."

"Please."

Chris took the bill from her hand. "I appreciate it. And it's nice meeting you like this."

She looked to her right and watched as a United 737 landed on the runway, roaring as it decelerated. "You never know who you'll run into, eh?" And then she walked away. Chris watched her disappear into the terminal, and he shook his head at the absurdity of even this world. Cate-fucking-Blanchett.

"You don't think there's reasons for things?"

Chris sat at the card table in the kitchenette, chewing a bite of his cheesesteak. Tammy'd had it delivered and she was still there and in her underwear. There were worse things to come home to.

"You don't think it means something, her coming over to you like that?"

"Jealous?" Chris said.

"Oh, please."

"What could it mean?"

"I don't know. Something."

"A famous actress tipped the gasman. That's what it means."

"Not just her," Tammy said. "Like everything, everyone. Doesn't all of this feel like it's going somewhere?"

Chris spoke around the food in his mouth. "Not on purpose." He swallowed. "And maybe nowhere good."

Tammy dropped her smile. Chris took a swig of beer and another bite. "You ever hear of parallel dimensions?" he asked.

That got her. She grinned and leaned across the table toward him. "Say what now?"

"Parallel dimensions. Multiple worlds."

"Okay."

"What if I told you I can move through them?"

"Is this like a symbol kind of thing? Like you're saying move through worlds, but you mean something else?"

"No. I literally travel to different worlds. Sometimes worlds like this, sometimes—not."

She plucked his arm. "Cate Blanchett was in that Thor movie with the different worlds. With the trash world."

Chris nodded. "I've been to one of those."

Tammy trailed her finger up to Chris's shoulder.

"Once a year, on my birthday—poof. I'm gone. Sayonara."

Tammy stood up then and grabbed the wrappers from their sandwiches. "This is dopey. You've been huffing fuel." She dropped the wrappers into the trashcan by the sink. "When's your birthday again?"

"August third. Midnight."

"Well, getting thrown around like that on your birthday sounds—hell, I'd take myself out, if not for my kids."

The statement hung between them for a moment, something she hadn't meant to say. Chris stared at her and she looked away. He wanted to tell her that he'd tried and that it hadn't worked. That he simply reset to the moments before he tried. But Chris didn't want to open Tammy's sadness more. "Worlds need people like you," he said, and that seemed to help.

"You're sweet." She leaned against him. "So, then if you're in a good world, like you are right now, you can just off yourself once a year."

Chris had tried that too. Even a good year on repeat was its own kind of hell.

"You could stay right here," she said, "with me." She ran her hand through Chris's hair, lowered to sit on his lap. "Could be romantic. Dark, but romantic."

And the idea was. The game they were playing. But the truth was that every year Chris became a new person, he felt farther away from a real one.

August 1, 3:51 A.M.

The wait was long for the agent. So many others had business with the quorum. The connection was weak, but the quorum was now online and aware of the agent's presence, and so the agent was at last able to disclose the details.

"The trail will not survive another journey, and so neither will the asset. Whatever occurred prior to the asset's arrival was damaging in ways we cannot yet estimate. We hope to bring the asset in."

"For what purpose?"

"We hope to uncover the nature of the asset's condition, which may prove useful to our cause."

"You are not a recruiter."

"The last world occupied by this asset is significant. The asset experienced a revelation there, we believe, making this one an anomaly—awakened, aware. Powerful. The trail tells us this."

"Tells your second, you mean."

"Jason, yes. I'm the one who discovered him all those years ago. Why do you not trust me?"

"It is our judgment that you seek the Simulacrum, not another agent."

"No."

"Why then reveal our presence to a clearly diminishing asset? In the midst of war, no less."

"It is our belief that the asset will prove useful. We cannot yet state how, but it is our belief. It has been too long since we encountered an anomaly. We can't let this one slip away."

"An anomalous trail is hardly cause for your fervor. There is no benefit or profit we can see."

"Our wait has been too long as well. Had you seen us earlier, we might have—the asset is now only a day from leaving."

"Is that all?"

"That is all."

"Then your request is denied. Cease all activity pertaining to the aforementioned asset and await further instruction regarding new orders."

"The asset—the anomaly—will not survive. Nor will any relevant data. This is a waste."

"You have your orders."

"But—"

"You have your orders."

Now

The AC in the van is beginning to dry his eyes. He blinks and squeezes them shut and opens them again. "I said I was expecting you. Aren't you curious how?"

"We assume it has something to do with the unstable world you escaped. The one that revealed you as a potential anomaly. I'm more curious why you won't tell us about that world."

"I'll tell you," he says. "I just—honestly, this isn't how I saw it happening. I expected someone. But definitely not you."

August 2, 11:03 P.M.

It was almost time. Chris looked at his watch—11:03 P.M. In the final moments, he would execute his plan and his long suffering would at last come to an end.

He walked from the GA terminal into the employee parking lot, looking up at the full moon. He stopped and stared in the way UFO victims do, waiting for the levitation, the great beam of light, and so Chris missed the true seizure coming. Black fabric was thrown over his face as someone grabbed both of his arms, hauling him backward. He was thrown into a vehicle, and he could hear a door rolling closed.

"What is this?" he said. "Hey, wha—who is this? What're you doing?" But no one answered.

He was in what he assumed was a van. He'd tried to work off the hood, but it was no use. They'd managed to bind his wrists with zip-ties and the plastic had worked its way under his watch and into his skin.

Chris was alone, and his kidnappers had been kind enough to leave the engine running with the AC on high. He smelled jet-fuel from his clothes and his own wet breath in the fabric of the hood. Chris heard sounds of movement from somewhere outside, voices. But he wasn't worried. Chris had been expecting this for some time.

The door dragged open then and the humidity hit him and the sweet smell of perfume. It closed again and the hood was removed. And there she was. His glamorous captor. Cate-fuck-ing-Blanchett.

She grinned. "Never know who you'll run into, eh?"

Now

She smiles and looks into his eyes. Cate Blanchett is looking into his eyes and Chris nearly gives in. He wants to drop everything and follow her, let her jab him with needles, fill him with tubes. She's Cate-fucking-Blanchett.

"But even if it's you," Chris says, "I have other plans."

"What plans?"

"The world I came from, the unstable one—I learned things there." Cate Blanchett leans toward him and it's dizzying to have her attention. "I say learn, but it's more sensory than that. I sort of—became aware of things."

"Became aware of what? Traveling?"

"Sure, yeah."

"And?"

"It's a lot to lay on you. It's heavy." He looks at his watch. Only a minute left. "The thing you're looking for, the thing in charge. I saw it. Well, I didn't see so much as recognize. And I nearly took in all the hows and the whys but they were so beyond me. Beyond you and your societies. Beyond all of us. But I found something else. I found an end."

L ̷ naik'ah 7, ∞ – Revelation

He was an awareness in the vacuum of space, a model of perhaps the greatest expansion of humanity in the scope of that universe. The achievement was considerable. They had evolved to at last pretend at immortality. They had wasted the world but saved their species so that biology was no longer necessary, and time held no more terror. They could travel the cosmos unhindered by it. And they had come so far that now the death of that universe was upon them, him, one of a few like him observing its final moments.

He was a witness. He wondered then if he was the only one. He had a year there, he knew, but he also knew that time meant nothing to him in that place, so it may as well have been seconds, years, ages.

A nearby moon reddened in the event horizon's approach, the threat of inertia in a universe governed by force and motion, gravity that would be still soon. If soon had meaning to one such as he. Or perhaps that was not the fate of that universe, only that of the there and then. Rather than being consumed by black holes, stars and stellar corpses might be flung into intergalactic space, set adrift in the void for as long as existence exists. Who could say?

He made his way to the lip of the great verge and peered without eyes beyond it. He did not see into a place from which light could not escape, but he had a sense of something on the other side staring back at him. He was overwhelmed by senses that had been distilled into his consciousness, no longer constrained by neural networks or the long spaces in a body. And in that way and on that brink, he remembered the first life he was born to. The smell of his mother's breast and the taste of her milk. The smell of his father's hands every day in those immeasurable periods of expansion. His cells multiplied and his tissues grew exponentially, neurons increasing, fibers insulating to speed the electricity of his thoughts. He grieved their loss because he had been compelled to travel. He still would be. Whatever looked at him from beyond was responsible, he knew, and it must've felt his knowing, the heat of his indictment.

But there was more there. He also sensed an end to him, should he choose it. As he recalled his origins, he somehow spied in the matrix of his newborn mind a signal. It was a flaring thing on a timer set to the passage of his relative time, and always it triggered and he went and it triggered and he went, call it yearly, he went and went. But he could stop that timer on the horizon of his going, just as he was on that horizon then, going. The end was coming, and he was going.

August 2, 11:59 P.M. –Now

"It's always been there. I've always been able to switch it off."

Cate Blanchett frowns. "It just has to be in the last minute before you go?"

"Right."

"I suppose that confirms you're an anomaly."

"It does? Why?"

"The switch. It implies design, wouldn't you say?"

"I guess so."

"Why didn't you stop it then and there?" she asks.

"Whatever I was in that world, in that awful point of reckoning, I wasn't fast. But I woke up in this world with a plan."

"So, we're down to thirty seconds. What do you do?"

Chris checks his watch and sees that she's right. The man outside is looking through the window at him. "What I failed to mention is how this involves you. I learned a lot staring into that space, too much." He sits up in his seat more. "When I became aware, the magnitude of what that switch could do—it's no small decision. It's not just me shutting down, you know?"

"You're wasting time, Chris."

"It's not just me that goes."

"Who else goes? Me?"

"Yes, but not just you. The world I occupy. All of it, everyone."

"Goes where?"

"Who can say? Whatever designed the switch will probably clean this up, so what does it matter, right?"

"Wh—"

"And I want to stay with you, I do. But none of this is real, Cate Blanchett. Not to me. I mean, you're Cate-fucking-Blanchett in the back of a van with a knife. A trans-world secret agent no less. It's not real, I'm not real and neither are you. Even the first life I remember wasn't. My true life, the one I was born into, is gone, somewhere far behind me."

Cate Blanchett grabs both sides of Chris's head. She is so close. He breathes in her perfume.

"I'm sorry," he says. And he does not slip from the world. Neither does it slip from him. He flips the switch and it's as if nothing ever happened.

ACKNOWLEDGMENTS

MANY WORLDS is a shared speculative multiverse founded by Cadwell Turnbull and guided by a collective of authors. The Many Worlds Collective includes established and award-winning authors in the speculative writing community—novelists, short story writers, playwrights, poets, game writers, essayists, podcasters, and more. Stories span genres and settings, from hard sci-fi to far-flung fantasy, magical realism to dystopian fiction to pseudo myth to surreal memoir—and everything in between. Our tales are always singular yet forever intersecting with the unique and complex device we call the Simulacrum.

Selected stories are published on our website in text and fully-voiced audio versions at **manyworldsforum.com**.

CONTRIBUTORS

Cadwell Turnbull is the editor of *MANY WORLDS* and author of the science fiction novels *The Lesson* and *No Gods, No Monsters*. His short fiction has appeared in *The Verge, Lightspeed, Nightmare, Asimov's Science Fiction*, and several anthologies, including *The Best American Science Fiction and Fantasy 2018* and *The Year's Best Science Fiction and Fantasy 2019*. His novel *The Lesson* was the winner of the 2020 Neukom Institute Literary Award. It was also shortlisted for the VCU Cabell Award, and longlisted for the Massachusetts Book Award. His novel *No Gods, No Monsters* was the winner of the Lambda Literary Award for Best LGBTQ Speculative Fiction, a finalist for the Locus Award for Best Fantasy Novel, and was longlisted for the PEN Open Book Award. Turnbull lives in Raleigh and teaches at North Carolina State University.

Justin C. Key is a speculative fiction writer and psychiatrist whose short stories have appeared in *The Magazine of Fantasy & Science Fiction, Strange Horizons, Tor.com, Escape Pod*, and *Lightspeed*. A graduate of Clarion West, his debut short story collection *The World Wasn't Ready For You* is forthcoming from HarperCollins. When Justin isn't writing, working with patients, or exploring Los Angeles with his wife, he's chasing after his three young (and energetic!) children. You can follow his journey at justinckey.com and @JustinKey_MD on Twitter.

K. W. Onley is a speculative fiction writer living in Massachusetts. You can find her on Twitter at @KayWOnley.

M. Darusha Wehm is the Nebula Award-nominated and Sir Julius Vogel Award winning author of the interactive fiction game *The Martian Job*, as well as the science fiction novels *Beautiful Red*, *Children of Arkadia*, *The Voyage of the White Cloud*, and the Andersson Dexter cyberpunk detective series. Their mainstream books include the Devi Jones' Locker Young Adult series and the humorous coming-of-age novel *The Home for Wayward Parrots*. Darusha's short fiction and poetry have appeared in many venues, including *Terraform* and *Nature*. Originally from Canada, Darusha lives in Wellington, New Zealand after spending several years sailing the Pacific.

Rebekah Bergman is the author of the novel *The Museum of Human History* (Tin House, 2023). Her fiction has been published in *Joyland*, *Tin House*, *The Masters Review Anthology*, and other journals. She lives in Rhode Island with her family.

Craig Lincoln is a writer of science fiction and fantasy and a graduate from North Carolina State University, earning an MFA in Fiction. He has held a myriad of odd jobs, including but not limited to: bus boy, projectionist, cruise ship janitor, fast food worker, and an airplane refueler. His fiction has been published in places such as *Daily Science Fiction* and *The Drabblecast*. He currently resides in Durham, North Carolina with his wife, two kids, and one dog. You can find him on Twitter @craigabyte or at craig-lincoln.com.

Josh Eure is a graduate of the North Carolina State University MFA program. His stories have won *Asimov's* Dell Award and the Brenda L. Smart Prize and reached the finalist list in Glimmer Train's Short Story Award for New Writers. He has also won Sundress Publications' Best of the Net Award for 2010 and has appeared in *Oxford American*, *James Gunn's Ad Astra*, *Surreal South*, *Southern Cultures*, *Raleigh Review*, and *Not One of Us*, among others. He was a finalist for the Piedmont Laureate in 2014. He is currently shopping a novel. He lives outside of Raleigh, NC with his wife and two children.

Theodore McCombs is a writer and environmental lawyer in San Diego. His debut short story collection, *Uranians* (Astra House Books) will appear in spring 2023. His fiction and essays have featured in *Best American Science Fiction & Fantasy 2019*, *Guernica*, *The Magazine of Fantasy & Science Fiction*, *Lightspeed Magazine*, *Nightmare Magazine*, *Lit Hub*, *Electric Literature*, and *Beneath Ceaseless Skies*, among others. He is a 2017 graduate of the Clarion Science Fiction & Fantasy Writers Workshop. Find him at theodoremccombs.com, on Twitter @mrbruff, or on Instagram @theodore.mccombs.

Cliff Winnig writes science fiction, fantasy, and horror. His short fiction has appeared on the *Escape Pod* podcast and in magazines and anthologies, including *Mad Scientist Journal*, *Footprints* (Hadley Rille Books), and *Straight Outta Deadwood* (Baen Books). He is a graduate of the Clarion Science Fiction and Fantasy Writers' Workshop. When not writing, Cliff plays sitar, studies aikido and tai chi, sings in a choral group, and does social dance, including ballroom, swing, and Argentine tango. He lives with his family in Silicon Valley, which constantly inspires him to think about the future. He can be found online at cliffwinnig.com.

Ben Murphy lives in North Carolina with his wife and a small menagerie. After a brief but fulfilling career as an unsuccessful rock star, he turned to writing. A graduate of the MFA program at North Carolina State University, where he now teaches composition, he is at work on a novel.

ABOUT THE PUBLISHER

Radix Media is a worker-owned printer and publisher based in Brooklyn, New York, producing beautifully designed books and ephemera. They publish new ideas and fresh perspectives, prioritizing the voices of typically marginalized communities to get to the root of the human experience.

Their books have won awards from *Foreword Reviews* and AIGA.

Find all of their books at **radixmedia.org/our-books**.

COLOPHON

This book was printed with union labor by Radix Media in Brooklyn, New York, using an AB Dick 9995 offset press.

The interior stock is Mohawk Via Vellum 70# text. The cover was printed on 100# cover stock using a Heidelberg Windmill letterpress.

OTHER TITLES BY RADIX MEDIA

Is This How You Eat a Watermelon?
Zein El-Amine

Mortals
John Dermot Woods & Matt L.

Fanning the Flames: A Molly Crabapple Coloring Book
Molly Crabapple

The Solar Grid
Ganzeer

There Is Still Singing in the Afterlife
JinJin Xiu

BINT
Ghinwa Jawhari

We Are All Things
Elliott Colla & Ganzeer

Futures: A Science Fiction Series
Various

Be the Change! A Justseeds Coloring Book
Justseeds Artists' Cooperative, ed. Molly Fair

Aftermath: Explorations of Loss & Grief
Anthology, ed. Radix Media